HER QUARANTINED COWBOY

KATHY FAWCETT

CHAPTER 1

he automatic doors of the hospital *whooshed* closed behind her, and Kat took a deep breath. Hearing that familiar sound made her blood pressure start to stabilize.

"Easy girl," she counseled herself as she walked slowly and deliberately across the tiles. "Just put one foot in front of the other."

She didn't think Gunnar West was looking at her backside from his pickup truck in the parking lot. But if he happened to be watching her navigate the shiny lobby floor in her little dress and pointy heels, she didn't want to give him the pleasure of seeing her trip and fall on her face—again.

One humiliating episode on a blind date was all Kat could take.

With each measured step, she hoped to regain a little more control over her life, and shut out the world once again.

Then Kat could begin to forget the cowboy she wished she never met.

CHAPTER 2

*J*osh Quell wanted to intercept his boss near the hospital entrance to hand her a medical chart and lab coat. He was glad he thought to bring Kat a cover up, especially after his eyes unwillingly looked down and widened in shock.

"Here I am," Kat reached her chief intern after tottering through the lobby doors.

Of all nights! Josh shook his head.

Kat Tate, infectious disease specialist, wasn't dressed anything like an expert in her field. Instead, she reminded Josh of that one girl who shows up at every wedding, looking like a neon sign that reads, "I'm single!" The girl who jumps the highest for the bouquet and hoots the loudest when the dee jay plays the song about *puttin' a ring on it.*

Josh had seen variations of that girl at a dozen events back in Iowa, where he grew up, but never thought he'd be working for her. This was a new side of Doctor Tate, one he could go a long time without seeing again.

He wished she would put the lab coat on instead of letting it hang over her arm, because her dress was tight and busting at the glittery seams with each step they took. But his call to her had been urgent, leaving no time for Kat to run home and change.

"You and the um... *girls* were on a date, I take it?" Josh glanced sideways at his boss.

Kat frowned.

"I guess it was a date," she said, tugging the little dress up with her free hand.

"Sorry you had to cut it short," he said.

"That's okay," she said, "you helped avert a homicide."

"Oh?"

"I was about to strangle the guy."

"That bad?"

"That bad," she said.

Josh walked with a sense of purpose and Kat worked hard to keep up. It didn't look easy in her Louboutin pumps.

"As soon as I get a minute," she said, "I'll slip into scrubs and the pair of runners I have in my locker."

Kat insisted that her priority was not the blister forming on her left foot, or the thorn-in-her-side cowboy who made her night miserable. It was their elderly patient, Belle Wild. The fact that Belle was getting worse instead of better told them something was seriously wrong.

"I never should have left the hospital tonight," she said, reading the chart.

"We have a handful of new patients, too," Josh said. "Admitted while you were at dinner, with similar symptoms."

"Whatever is making these patients sick is dangerous and spreading fast," Kat said.

CHAPTER 3

at would have to make a quick prognosis so she could alert Shep Arndt, the director of the hospital, and the man who hired her out of big city obscurity.

"Come be a prestigious big fish in a decidedly smaller pond," he said, with the promise that she could help create a new Infectious Disease department from the ground up. "We're not too small to matter, I'll tell you that," he continued. "Our hospital is new and our county is growing like crazy. You'll be getting in on the ground floor, Kat."

The charming Arndt had sold hard, but Kat wasn't a hard sell. She was ready for a leadership role, and there were way too many layers of specialists standing between her and the coveted director position in Chicago.

She was ready for a change of scenery, in a community where she could afford to buy a house and not just throw rent after a tiny apartment with rusty pipes and frozen windows. Kat dreamed that someday she'd have the picket fence lifestyle—a quiet place where she could have a cat and bake pies.

Of course, with her westward move, she might have to adjust her fence from a picket style to a split rail. But the bump in pay, coupled with a lower cost of living, was like winning the lottery. She could finally whittle down the last of her debt.

"Full disclosure," Arndt had said, "winters in Wyoming, well, they can be harsh."

Kat laughed at that, and told him about the notorious Chicago winters, with winds howling in off of Lake Michigan. "How much worse could winter be?"

It was his turn to laugh. "Winter in Wyoming is like a bad mother-in-law—it arrives unannounced and stays long past its welcome," he said.

Overall, his sales pitch appealed to her Midwest sensibilities. After a little negotiation, Kat said "yes" to the West Gorge Medical Center in West Gorge, Wyoming.

So far, her work had been quiet, allowing her to get her footing at the new hospital. Tonight, she would earn her salary. Decisions would have to be made—unpopular ones. And there was no one to hide behind. If this illness turned out to be what Kat suspected, there was only one way to contain the spread.

Shep would flip out.

"On the bright side, you smell delicious," Josh said. "What is that?"

"A combination of perfume, the pasta I was about to eat," Kat said, "and a little dab of disappointment behind each ear."

Josh nodded as they walked.

"Did you get it to go?"

"The disappointment, or the pasta?"

"I think I already know that answer," he said.

They reached the elevator and stopped. Kat opened Belle's chart and looked down. She frowned at her snug bodice, barely contained in her tight blue cocktail dress. Her snowy skin was red and irritated from the sequins and sparkling trim.

"Maybe this dress was a bit too... big city." Kat's voice sounded deflated and her shimmery bare shoulders fell in defeat. She looked up at Josh, one of the only friends she had in town. "Should I have worn jeans and spurs or something?"

Josh shrugged. He was new to Wyoming, too.

SINCE ARRIVING THE MONTH BEFORE, KAT HAD VENTURED INTO TOWN only a time or two. She enjoyed window shopping at the art galleries, but didn't notice any clothing stores in West Gorge. Nothing like the *haute couture* window displays on Chicago's Miracle Mile—with rail-thin mannequins being choked to death by tight collars and pinched waistlines.

In the season's hottest colors, of course.

In West Gorge, they had outfitters that sold everything from canvas tarps to bear repellent. In the windows, curvy mannequins wore fringed jackets and tight blouses with pearl buttons, faded jeans and pointy-toed boots.

One plastic woman had a pick ax leaning against her leg and a lasso rope over her shoulder. Apparently, she was going to rope cattle and mine ore after putting dinner on the table.

The rustic fashions were fun to look at, but Kat never expected West Gorge women to actually dress like Calamity Jane for a night out. She planned on going "full Chicago" in a cocktail dress and heels for her first date in town.

The thought of dressing up made Kat happy. That is, until she saw her date's reaction and realized her efforts had been wasted on the Neanderthal cowboy that one of her favorite co-workers, nurse Jackie, had insisted she meet.

"What's wrong with him?"

Jackie's mouth fell open at the question, but Kat stood her ground. She believed that when it came to men, the really good ones were already off the market. And the iffy ones, the damaged goods, well those men needed to be set up by friends on blind dates.

"There's not a single thing wrong with Gunnar West," Jackie insisted with pure indignation in her voice. "He's tall, he's nice, and that's all you need to know. He will pick you up here at six o'clock. I want to hear everything on Monday."

Jackie was happily married to Red Carter, her high school sweetheart.

Kat knew that Jackie seated guests at Red's Rib Shack, her husband's restaurant, on weekends. She also helped Red make batch after succulent batch of his secret BBQ sauce.

"You come by any time, Kat," Jackie said, "and we'll fatten up those bones."

What Kat didn't know was that Jackie was one of the few women in West Gorge who had not dated Gunnar West—though it was clear she thought the world of him.

Jackie would definitely hear everything, Kat thought. She'd get an earful.

"Tall? Sure he was tall! He wore cowboy boots and a big stupid hat on his head," Kat couldn't wait to tell her. "He was put out that I wanted to eat at the Italian bistro, then mad that the maître d' asked him to remove his hat. But would he leave it on the coat rack like a normal man? *Oh no!* He had to place it on the little romantic dining table with the candle in the center, where it almost knocked over my soup."

Kat decided quickly that the self-absorbed Gunnar West, with his scowl and his clumsy cowboy ways, could never be the *plus one* she had been looking for. The gentleman who would come with her to the many weddings and dinners Kat was invited to; a man who knew enough to compliment a pretty dress when he saw one.

Gunnar didn't even seem all that impressed that she was a doctor —a specialist, at that—who had been wooed by the town of West Gorge. If he read the article about her in the *West Gorge Weekly*, he didn't say.

He was intimidated. That's what he was, Kat was certain.

She watched Gunnar sigh and roll his eyes at the fancy lobster ravioli served in brown butter, and decided he must be used to a lower class of food. And women. Maybe he preferred dating hash slingers at the local diner. Maybe he was looking for a girlfriend who would help him feed his cows and muck the stalls at his ranch.

Free labor, that's what he wanted. Not a specialist in epidemics, pandemics and infectious diseases—with several articles published in medical journals.

Well, Gunnar West was an infectious disease that Kat fully intended to avoid catching at all costs. His attitude tonight had been vaccine enough—just a little dose of the illness itself to make her completely immune going forward. She would wash her hands of him for a full two minutes, while singing *Goodbye Cowboy, Goodbye*. And watch his germs go down the drain.

AFTER CHECKING ON BELLE AND THE NEW PATIENTS, KAT GAVE ORDERS to the nurses and interns.

"For now, no one leaves this wing and no new visitors," she said to the wide-eyed nods of a staff accustomed to the free rein of this touchy-feely little community. Unlike the big city hospital, people here came and went as they pleased, with little regard to rules or hours of visitation.

Lab results would prove her theory within the hour and she asked Josh to personally shepherd them to her. In the meantime, Kat focused on the cascading decisions facing her on this otherwise unremarkable Friday night. If her suspicions were right, and she thought they were, she would have to follow a swift protocol.

Should she consult with her former boss? As head of infectious diseases for the large hospital in Chicago, he'd be a great sounding board. But no, she couldn't go running back to daddy—not after stepping out on her own.

The test results would be all the daddy she needed.

She'd call Shep Arndt first and apprise him of the situation.

"It's a Code Q, Shep," she'd say. "Full quarantine for everyone between the main entrance and the north wing, for seven days."

Then she'd call the CDC and get ready for the muck in her own stall to hit the fan.

Now, where was her phone?

CHAPTER 4

*H*ospitals were stressful places for many, but not for Doctor Kat Tate. Her college roommates used to brag about feeling *Zen* walking into their yoga studios and smelling the lemongrass incense. That's how Kat felt about hospitals.

"Ah, my inner sanctum," Kat would think, getting that first whiff of Lysol.

Her mother would find it odd—and sad—that her only child felt more at home in a clinical environment than she'd ever felt at the little house in Illinois, where she grew up. But to Kat, hospitals just made more sense. The life and death dramas that played out could be charted and therefore explained. More so than the never-ending dramas that played out between her parents in the little house.

She rarely visited.

Kat told her mother she had to work most holidays, which was true, but only because she volunteered. She also told her mother that she slept better at the overpriced efficiency walk-up where she lived, in Chicago.

Her mother said she understood, and perhaps she did. Maybe she knew that Kat avoided any place considered "home," where her heart was supposed to be, and was resolved to carry this sense of detachment everywhere she went.

She was successful, until she stepped foot in Wyoming.

Years before, when Kat was an intern, Rod Baylor, the iconic lead singer for *Fitch Band*, was put under a super-secret quarantine at the hospital. He returned from an overseas tour with a highly contagious virus that Kat's team had to treat and contain.

The hospital swarmed with agents for the band who pressed the doctors not to talk to reporters. None had—but every single one of them except Kat walked around star struck at their brush with fame, with eyes bugging out and mouths gaping open.

She knew that's how she looked when she first saw Wyoming. Star struck. Her suspicions were confirmed when she caught her reflection in the mirrored aviator sunglasses worn by the driver who picked her up at the airport.

Kat was gaping like a codfish, and didn't care.

She couldn't find the words to describe the layers of beauty she saw from the window—the mountain peaks against a backdrop of azure blue skies, the lines of pines and other tall trees, and the deep gorge that cut through the foothills and held a flowing, winding river.

"Do I look up at the hills, or down at the gorge?" She asked from the back seat.

"Yes," the driver answered, amused.

The rugged and complex scenery captivated the stunned doctor. In spite of her resolution to remain indifferent, something began unravelling in her tightly wound heart.

THE HOSPITAL OFFERED TO PUT HER UP FOR THREE MONTHS WHILE SHE looked for her own place, and she gladly accepted. Kat expected a utilitarian room with a kitchenette and that would have been fine. But her new home left her even more speechless than the scenery.

Kat couldn't believe her eyes when she first walked into apartment #22 of the Gorge View Condominiums and saw vaulted beamed ceilings, leather sofas, and oversized picture windows that framed the mountains.

In the open kitchen, double stainless-steel ovens were tucked into a brick wall. And shiny granite countertops held a gift basket of fruit, cheese, scones and freshly ground coffee.

Following the apartment complex manager, JaneAnn, like an eager puppy, Kat padded on thick carpets into the main suite to see a large bed made up with soft Turkish linens. A free-standing soaker bathtub sat in a coved window that overlooked the gorge.

JaneAnn proceeded to show Kat how to operate the remote blinds in the bedroom and all three wall-mount TVs.

"There must be some mistake," she told JaneAnn uneasily at the end of the tour. "Obviously, this place is for somebody important. I'm just a nobody from the Midwest."

"You may be nobody there, Doctor Tate, but you're somebody to West Gorge," JaneAnn smiled. "It's paid up for three months and you can stay longer. Just give me a holler."

Paid up for three months—the words swirled in Kat's head long after JaneAnn was gone. "How could that be?" Kat wanted to ask. She'd never been handed anything; had to work for everything since the age of 14, when her father walked out on her family.

That was twenty years ago.

Yet here she was, being handed a beautifully furnished apartment with a roomy balcony overlooking the hills.

The first few days, Kat ping-ponged between feelings of euphoria and certainty that someone made a mistake. It was just a matter of time before she'd be found out and kicked out, she was sure. She kept her suitcase half packed for the embarrassing eviction. "You were right—you *don't* belong here!" JaneAnn would then walk Kat to a small basement apartment with an egress window and a hot plate.

After a few weeks went by and she was still at #22, Kat hung up her last few things and shoved the suitcase under the bed.

Every morning in Wyoming was as exciting as her first. She'd wake up at early light and watch the snow-capped mountains come into focus. Taking a carafe of coffee out on the balcony, along with a scone and a wool throw from the great room, Kat would settle into an oversized log rocking chair for as long as possible before getting ready for work.

Without blaring, angry car horns, or trains zooming by, Kat could hear birds. She could make out the sound of water rushing through the gorge. When she had time, she grabbed the binoculars off the burled walnut coffee table to search for eagle nests and baby foxes.

Accustomed to holding her breath while walking through the smog and soot of the city, Kat took deep gulps of fresh mountain air until she felt lightheaded.

"Wyoming," Kat said between warm sips of coffee, "where have you been all my life?"

The month of June came and went and Kat started to relax and feel at home. She spoke with JaneAnn and realized that with her new salary, she could easily afford to extend the lease and stay if she wanted to.

For the first time in her life, Kat Tate had a home she wanted to go home to every night—but tonight was not going to be that night.

CHAPTER 5

*G*unnar West finally got back home to his ranch, but not before driving through his favorite greasy spoon and picking up a double order of burgers and fries. That little Eye-*talian* meal, or what he managed to choke down before his so-called date got called back to work, was like a little tease to his manly pallet.

Instead of being disappointed that their evening was cut off—and maybe he should have pretended to be—he was openly relieved, and sure Kat saw it on his face. Gunnar didn't care. He knew it was going to be a rotten night as soon as he drove up and saw her standing by the hospital entrance.

"*Please*, let that not be her." He said this out loud as he pulled up in his favorite pickup and caught his date's unappreciative look, aimed at his ride of choice.

"What's her deal?" Gunnar knew that every inch of the tall truck's paint and shiny trim had been washed and waxed. He even polished the leather interior.

But she did not hide her disdain.

She had some paint and shiny trim on her too, Gunnar noted, shaking his head in wonder. *What was Jackie thinking with this one?*

Standing out like a sore thumb and dressed like an off-brand Barbie, his date wore a short glittery dress and stood unsteadily on shoes that would never do for walking along the river.

Gunnar was the first to admit he didn't have a lot of dating tools in his toolbox, so the moonlit path along the river was always a safe bet. It was secluded enough for a clandestine kiss or two, and perfect for walking off the shared BBQ rack at Red's Rib Shack.

"You can tell everything you need to know about a woman by the way she eats ribs," he told his dad, Ridge West, before heading out. Ridge had been sitting at the granite island of the massive ranch kitchen. In front of him was a white ironstone platter with samples of the many dishes that their cook, Justice, pulled from the oven.

Justice Kemp had come to help the busy West family for a spell after the youngest brother, Colton, was born, nearly thirty years before. After tasting a few of his meals, Gunnar's mother, Randi, wouldn't let Justice leave. She had two energetic boys under foot plus a newborn, a sprawling ranch home that was being constructed, and the West Foundation to run.

The Wests also regularly fed hungry ranch hands and hosted many visitors.

"Give the man whatever he wants," Randi had reportedly said to her husband, with a child in each arm and another clinging to her leg.

Ridge quickly had plans drawn up to build a cook house on the property with an apartment for Justice. The new cook house boasted a wall of ovens, freezers, and other restaurant-grade appliances—all of which Justice kept employed for countless events on the ranch, and years of family gatherings.

These days were quieter.

Now, Justice preferred to do his cooking in the Big House, as he called the main lodge, to fill the walls with the good aromas the West men had grown up with. And just maybe, Gunnar suspected, to keep Ridge from getting lonely.

Today, he was assembling large pans of hearty dishes along with the "vegetable forward" sides insisted upon by Gunnar's mother. Though Randi was gone, she had extracted a promise from Justice that he would take care of the men in her absence and not let them "go to pot" by eating takeout pizzas and drive-through burgers.

"And for goodness sakes, Justice," she reportedly said to the cook, "when the church ladies start bringing over that endless parade of potato-chip casseroles, please make the boys eat a salad along with them."

To the cook, Randi's marching orders were just shy of the spoken word of God, and nevermore was a meal served without something green and leafy.

"I'm not sure your theory about the ribs is definitive, Gunnar," Ridge laughed between bites of lasagna, baked chicken and kale salad, "but it's a good start."

Gunnar stood firm in his conviction. He wanted a woman who wasn't afraid to pick up a slathered and saucy rib with her bare hands. A fork was a deal breaker. And if she took more than her fair share of the rack, or tried to? That was the glass slipper he'd been waiting to find.

"I hope she has an *appetite*," Gunnar told his dad, and he was out the door.

On the way to his date, Gunnar West thought about this last comment. He did want a woman with an appetite, but not just for ribs. For life, for love, for nature and the world around them. He wanted someone to challenge him the way his mother used to challenge his father before she passed away.

He himself was hungry—starving—for someone who would expect more of him. To keep him on his toes and keep him honest. Gunnar wasn't getting any younger, he knew, and decided he was finally ready for one woman to hold onto. Someone who wanted to hold onto him.

Darlene Shire came as close as any to being that woman, until she took herself out of the running. Much to Gunnar's surprise. For two full years of ups and downs, they made a go of it. Darlene could fill out a pearl-buttoned western shirt, put away a rack of ribs, and hold her own in a line dance. But Gunnar couldn't deny that all too quickly, their interests began diverging.

They started arguing about stupid stuff in some of his favorite locations along the river and in the mountains—places that were sacred to Gunnar. Places he didn't want to sully with unpleasant memories of raised voices. They were also openly bickering in public.

"She likes the *idea* of you Gunnar," his brother, Pike, observed, "but she doesn't seem to like you as you are. Or the rest of us for that matter."

Gunnar didn't take it well when Pike said that. A man of few words, Pike spent too much time observing, and Gunnar always bristled at being on his brother's radar. But now, in the rear-view mirror, he could see that Pike was right. Darlene always wanted him to be different. She wanted to change everything to suit her vision.

Many things in her life were "something she could work with," especially him.

Still, Gunnar was antsy and ready to lay down his wild ways. He figured that if he committed more fully to Darlene, their marriage would be something she could work with.

He wasn't perfect, he knew, and maybe the perfect woman simply didn't exist. Like a game of horseshoes, maybe love was getting as close as you could and making the best of things. If he and Darlene could just jump in with their boots on, he thought, they could build an imperfect but happy life together.

The Wild West was tamed by men and women who barely knew each other when they married, like his great-grandparents. He imagined they were like most couples in the 1800s, so busy staying alive and storing up food for the long Wyoming winters that they didn't have time to argue and fight like he and Darlene.

Gunnar was always busy with the ranch, one of the largest in the state, and with the family's charitable foundation. He also sat on the board of the hospital. Gunnar accepted that whoever he married might also be busy with her career, in addition to their children.

Ideally, she would take on some of his mother's charitable works.

Randi had been a corporate attorney when she met Ridge West all those years ago, and never slowed down. Ridge used to joke that "Randi had three boys, but her *baby* was the West Foundation."

Diverting some of the West family's many millions, Randi began methodically pouring into the community through the foundation, and into the people who settled into West Gorge. All while helping Ridge run the ranch and raising their three sons.

It was easy to idealize his mother now that she was gone, but Randi and Ridge's marriage had its moments, he knew. Gunnar remembered the two of them trading angry looks. And a few family dinners where the boys kept their hands near their plates, lest they get shot by the slings and arrows flying back and forth between his parents' eyes.

But such moments were rare.

There were far more tender touches and quiet whispers not meant for young ears. Gunnar remembered wandering to the kitchen late at night once as an adolescent, and seeing his parents slowly dancing together by the light of the great room fireplace.

And there were many nights when Ridge and Randi would smile at each other and turn in early, telling the boys to get their homework done and do the same.

Did it really matter who a man married as long as that someone was equally committed to weathering both good times and bad? Gunnar wasn't sure. But more and more, he could see his chance to find out slipping away. Darlene, the unassuming girl he thought he knew, wanted something else. She wanted fame and fortune as a writer and reporter—though Gunnar thought the West fortune should be enough for just about anyone.

"I would be thrilled to have the West name, Gunnar," she once said before he'd actually popped the question, "but I want to make a name for myself first. And not just with our small-town newspaper."

And she did, sort of. First as a stringer to the bigger papers, and then through feature articles about ranch life written for an audience of city dwellers.

"It's what their itching ears want to hear," Ridge had chuckled when he read them.

Gunnar knew that through the food channels and reality television shows, people had started to romanticize the country and western lifestyle. "If they only knew how much work this simple life takes to maintain," he laughed with his father, "they'd high tail it back to the city."

Still, Gunnar thought he and Darlene could be happy together at least some of the time, if each of them would lay down a little bit of their stubbornness.

"You should have a life in addition to the West Ranch," Gunnar assured Darlene.

But Darlene wanted a life instead of the West Ranch.

When she got a chance to join the staff of the *Tri-City News*, she jumped at it without even talking it over with Gunnar. Before he could open his mouth to weigh in, Darlene was packed and saying her fond farewells.

"Just like that?" he asked, incredulous.

Darlene could only nod. She gave him a dry kiss on the cheek before driving off.

It hurt Gunnar that she kept him out of the loop and that he first heard the news from his youngest brother, Colton.

"Looks like Darlene got a better offer than you and West Gorge," Colton had said with a smirk. Unlike Pike, who weighed and measured every word, the more gregarious Colton never stopped to think before running off at the mouth. "*Hoo wee*, that girl dropped you like a hot potato!" Colton went on, as Gunnar tried to ignore him.

With Colton, it was best to let him run out of steam.

But if Gunnar was totally honest, it didn't hurt as badly as he thought it would. After the initial shock, he felt relief wash over him at having an easy way out of the often-suffocating nearness of Darlene Shire.

"Hurts more like a splinter than a thorn," he told his brothers, and shrugged.

And a splinter is forgotten in days.

By the time his friend, Jackie, called to ask if he would show the pretty new doctor in town the sights, it had been nearly six months since Darlene drove off to the bright lights of the big city. Gunnar was more than ready, he said.

Jackie knew him well and he trusted her. They grew up together in church, making faces behind the open hymnals when the youth pastor wasn't looking. Their mothers had been the best of friends, which would always raise Jackie's stock in his estimation.

But he couldn't wait to give her a call and ask what she had been thinking.

"I'm all for charity," he wanted to say, "but that girl, that charity case, is hopeless."

Of course, he'd keep those harsh thoughts to himself.

While he could never be mad at Jackie, he'd pull her chain a bit with this one. But bringing up charities would be crass. Everyone knew that his ancestors founded the town, naming it West Gorge after the deep chasm that time and swiftly flowing mountain water had cut into the hills. As one of the largest land owners in the county, in the state even, they had a civic responsibility to fund the schools, the businesses and the hospitals.

Randi and Ridge raised their sons to understand they were privileged, but that didn't excuse any of them from working hard. They just might have to work harder than most to be above reproach, his parents would say, and to set an example.

Gunner always knew much would be expected of him. But of all the selfless acts he'd done for the good of the community, escorting Doctor Kat Tate to a fussy little café, where he had to take his hat off to eat a girlie-sized portion of glorified spaghetti-o's, was asking too much.

CHAPTER 6

*G*unnar exhaled a loud sigh. He met his obligation and kept his word to Jackie. It was a relief to drive under the over-sized arches, emblazoned at the top with a hammered metal WR emblem for West Ranch. Everything as far as the eye could see belonged to the Wests and Gunnar was home. He would quickly forget the blind date, just as soon as he checked on his horse and pet his dog.

As if on cue, his dog, Jet, came barking alongside the truck as it rolled into the circle drive by the big lodge that was home—the lodge Ridge and Randi designed and had built from logs, timber and boulders.

The house was set into the hill like an iceberg, so the front entry-way, flanked with tall lodge-pole pines, remained unassuming in its scale. The unseen backside of the house, tucked into the hill below, is where the lodge exploded into multiple levels of wings and suites in addition to the big family kitchen, dining hall and great room.

Twenty-foot-high windows faced the mountains and the gorge, capturing views of wildlife and the streams that ran over fallen trees and rocks. Across from the circle drive, a 12-bay family garage held the West's fleet of trucks and cars. A few miles further up the ranch road, barns and other outbuildings housed livestock, horses, offices and equipment.

The property also boasted a cook house and a guest house. There were other, rustic buildings further back in the hills, including the original settler's cabin.

Gunnar enjoyed seeing the lodge at night, when the cast iron light fixtures tucked under the eaves shone softly on the yews and pines growing around the lodge.

"I'm home, Jet." Gunnar parked and opened the door to pat the excited dog on the head. "We dodged a bullet, boy." But in spite of the sour taste in his mouth from his disastrous date, he had to laugh at the memory of Kat Tate trying to climb into his tall truck.

"Shoulda' seen it, Jet," he smiled.

WHEN HE ARRIVED AT THE HOSPITAL PARKING LOT EARLIER, HE PRAYED to the gods of blind dates to please not let the overdressed beauty pageant contestant near the curb be his. Gunnar could tell by the way her glittering shoulders sagged that she was not thrilled either.

"Are you…" Gunnar spoke through his passenger window after parking in the pickup zone, unable to hide the disappointment in his voice. This woman would definitely *not* be the mother of his future children.

"Are you…" Kat said in response, with disappointments of her own.

Resigned, Gunnar touched the brim of his hat as a show of respect, and got out of the truck to help her into the front seat. As he walked around the back end, he looked longingly at the camping gear stashed in the bed, wishing he could make a run for the hills instead of doing what he was about to do.

His escape fantasy was interrupted by the sound of his passenger door opening and his date, who apparently had no patience, loudly exclaiming, "what the…"

Kat Tate had one high-heeled foot on the running board as she tried to get purchase. Her fancy shoe was sliding back and forth and she was in obvious distress.

"Ma'am," he said as he reached her, not knowing where to put his hands to help.

Her dress was as tight as it was short. With her leg on the running board, the dress had nowhere to go but up. She shot her arm high in search of a handle to grab onto, which only made things worse. The little dress she wore could only cover so much ground.

"*Please* let me help you," Gunnar pleaded, still not knowing exactly how.

Kat looked over her bare shoulder at him with the most beautiful and accusing eyes. Her face steamed with frustration at her predicament—she was stuck! Unable to go up or down.

Gunnar tried to not to smile but that was a tall order. It was the cutest thing he'd seen in a long time, and her rugged independence was sort of endearing. His date was pretty, that much was true. Long wavy hair hung down over her bare shoulders, each looking soft and silky to the touch. Maybe she had too much makeup on, but her smoky eyes sparked like fireworks in her anger and he was mesmerized.

"Just give me a little…" Kat insisted, not knowing how to finish the sentence.

A little what, Gunner thought, *a push, a pull, a shove, a kiss…*

Gunnar stood behind to shield her predicament from the growing number of parking lot onlookers. She had no idea just how much of herself she was putting on display, he was sure, and felt the urge to protect her.

"I think you ought to help the little lady, and fast," a woman said while walking to her car.

Gunnar shrugged helplessly. They were gaining an audience, though, and that wasn't good. Thankfully, nobody had their phone cameras out—yet. But it was probably the most exciting thing going on in West Gorge on this Friday night.

He made an executive decision to put an end to the street performance by assisting her into the truck from behind. He acted quickly. Placing his weathered hands on her rear, he gave a firm lift that left her no choice but to flop onto the front seat with a thud.

Gunnar had intended to keep his hands on the blue fabric of the dress, but may not have been completely successful in that. Still, he got the job done, and was proud of his own efficiency. He was also proud that, though tempted, he did *not* give her hind end a slap, as he surely would have if she were a calf going into a pen.

"Great," Kat groaned, laying disheveled on the leather front seat, "just great."

Gunnar slammed the truck door closed behind her, to the hoots and applause of onlookers.

"Let's move along, folks," he said, quietly, "nothing to see here." He took his time walking to his side of the truck, dreading what was in store for him.

By the time Gunnar got back around to the driver's side, Kat was sitting up straight and had tucked herself back into the little bit of fabric she thought was a dress. But then he noticed her purse had spilled onto the floor in the commotion.

"Should we..." Gunnar said hopelessly, gesturing to the mess.

"Can we... just... go...?" Kat was seething.

"Yes, ma'am," he said, and they drove off in silence.

Later, in the parking lot of the restaurant his date had insisted on, Gunnar helped Kat pick up the lipstick and wallet that tumbled out of her little purse. There was also a hospital ID and loose change. "I get the quarters," he joked, to an unreceptive audience.

Back at the ranch, Gunnar sat in his truck, thinking about the wildly unsuccessful blind date with the doctor, then shook his head to clear the memories. A few of the images he was certainly not meant to see. And there were definitely some things he had no right to touch.

But what was done was done.

As he was about to get out, Jet woofed at a buzzing sound coming from underneath the seat. Reaching down, he pulled out a ringing cell phone that was not his. Which could only mean one thing.

"Oh, for the love… her dang phone!" Gunnar reluctantly closed the door and turned the truck once again towards West Gorge and the hospital.

CHAPTER 7

"That ridiculous truck. There are garbage trucks in Chicago smaller than Gunnar's truck." Sitting in the doctor's lounge, Kat mumbled in frustration as she frantically searched her purse for her phone. She would need to stay connected to her boss and staff on what was shaping up to be a long night.

Everything had been retrieved after spilling her belongings, she was sure. Her call from Josh came in while she was dining—so where could her phone possibly be? It must have fallen again on the floor of Gunnar West's big fat truck, probably while scrambling to get in for the drive back to the hospital.

How did he expect her to get up on that seat with any dignity?

It must have been his plan to pull up in that dinosaur and use it as an excuse to put his caveman hands all over her. Did it occur to him she might be wearing a dress—did he think she'd be wearing daisy dukes and a bandana?

Kat's wardrobe was limited, she knew, but she had the basics covered. Scrubs, of course, one interview suit, and assorted cocktail gowns. Before this night, Kat thought she was ready for anything. It seemed she could dress for a Chicago wedding but not a Wyoming truck.

In hindsight, her tiny little dress of choice had been a disaster, giving the cowboy much more *hindsight* than she ever intended. When her expensive shoe became stuck on his running board, she couldn't go up or down. It would have been comical, except she was fighting mad over the predicament. Gunnar wasn't much help, even though he looked like a man who could do just about anything.

She almost felt bad for him.

There was one moment when Kat looked over her shoulder and right into Gunnar's eyes—he had beautiful, dark eyes—and it was obvious how embarrassed he was. The innocent confusion, the mischievous smile that played on his lips, these were almost charming; his helplessness beckoned her to him, in spite of her anger.

For a split second, she thought she and Gunnar might let their guard down and bust out laughing. Until he took matters into his own hands.

Literally!

While holding her gaze and completely disarming her, Gunnar West placed his rough hands on her rear—one hand here and one hand there—and pushed her up and onto the seat of the pickup with a *git 'er done* efficiency that shocked and alarmed her. Kat didn't see that move coming until all she could see was the seat of his truck.

After a few hard blinks, Kat got a hold of herself and sat up.

"Good grief, girl," she said to herself, shaking her head at the memory of his quick and powerful move. "Extravagant lengths to get some human contact!"

Clearly, he was used to dating a different type of woman. It was obvious that her class and education made them wholly incompatible.

But those eyes... and those...

"Doctor Tate?"

"Those *hands*," Kat spoke involuntarily, before looking up and seeing her intern.

"Hands? Yes, I have the lab results in my hands." Josh Quell was handing her the folder that would determine her next step, her next week, and most likely her career.

"You'll want to see this," he said, somberly.

. . .

"*QUARANTINE?* THAT'S A SERIOUS WORD, KAT."

Shep Arndt had been called away from the final course of a romantic dinner with his wife, and didn't sound as though he welcomed the interruption.

"It's a serious and contagious virus, Shep." Kat ducked into an unused office off the lobby to make the phone call. "We currently have nine patients."

"Eleven now." Josh whispered an update.

"*Eleven* patients now in the north wing have tested positive," she continued. "For a small community, that's a big number. Everyone who has been exposed is at risk not only for themselves, but to everyone they've come in contact with."

When Shep was silent, Kat continued.

"If we contain it now, we can control the spread and the narrative, Shep," she said.

"And if we don't?" Shep asked.

"We risk lives and have a lot to answer for," Kat answered, "both locally and with the CDC—the Centers for Disease Control."

Shep Arndt was silent. This was completely new to him and he didn't want to have egg on his face if the new doctor was wrong. But if he ignored her and she was right...

"I know it's extreme, Shep, and you're worried it could cast the hospital in a negative light—but I see it as a positive, proactive decision," Kat said.

"I should come down to the hospital," Shep said.

"You should stay home," Kat said, "you are nearly sixty with asthma, and therefore a compromised immunity. I don't need you to be sick."

"Hmm. Okay, I'll call Buck Land, chief of hospital security," he said, nervously. "He and I will back you up with anything you need."

And then he said, "you call the shots Kat. Just make sure they're the right ones."

No pressure there, she thought, but calling these shots is what Kat had been preparing for her entire medical career.

"This is why you hired me, Shep," she said and hung up.

CHAPTER 8

 hen Kat decided years ago to specialize in disease control, her mentor in Chicago warned her it was not for the faint of heart.

"Prepare to be unpopular, highly doubted, second guessed, and called all sorts of names from crazy to paranoid and everything in between. You'll be hanged if you do and hanged if you don't. You'll be asked why you didn't you catch it sooner, and why you didn't wait a little longer, in the same breath."

And he was right. No specialist came out of an epidemic or pandemic smelling like a rose, especially now that everyone had access to the almighty internet and could find their own version of the truth.

During an infectious disease event, everyone was suddenly an expert and a critic.

But Kat Tate had trained for this. She was ready to bet her entire career that closing off the north wing of the hospital was the right thing to do.

"She who hesitates risks lives," she said out loud to bolster her own courage, and walked with a purposeful stride in her heels towards the hospital entrance. Buck Land would be waiting for her in an adjacent wing with a team of people, all appearing very official and at-the-ready with their walkie-talkies.

To his credit, Buck was all business. The askance look he gave her as she strode into the room wearing her cocktail dress was barely perceptible.

"We'll have two people on the inside and two more on the outside of the double sliding doors, Doctor Tate," Buck said. "There are about forty people in the north wing—consisting of a few visitors and patients, and then various medical and non-medical staff."

While listening, Kat's stomach began rolling around in a great jumble of nerves.

Was she crazy? Was she doing the right thing? Only time would tell and it was too late to back down now. Her every instinct told her to run through the double doors while there was still time and make a dash back to the anonymous city, where she could blend in again.

"We will go live in ten minutes," Buck continued, and they all looked up at the clock on the wall. It was ten minutes before nine o'clock at night.

The public relations team was crafting a statement to send to the press, Kat knew, and soon she would be called on to make a statement that would be streamed live.

"All of your needs will be met during your quarantine—and that goes for everyone," Buck said. "There are plenty of rooms and beds. You and your team will determine how people are separated from each other."

People would be shocked and angry, Kat knew, from previous drills and real-life events. Some visitors would protest heavily, but if she was lucky, eventually they'd settle into a routine of watching TV while wearing scrubs, and eating pizza and ice cream sundaes delivered through the double sliding doors.

"A little comfort food can soothe many savage beasts, Buck," she said.

He nodded.

While they talked, Kat looked around the lobby at unsuspecting staff and visitors—people she would be locked in with over the next week. Nurses walked by in pairs, talking and laughing. A few people were on their phones, calling family with updates, no doubt. Two women in the hospital gift shop unpacked new items as they ate pizza.

A teenage boy in a bulky jacket walked past carrying a bouquet of flowers, seemingly looking for a room number; his grandma's room most likely. Kat hoped the boy didn't have any hot dates that he would have to cancel. Just because her love life was not going so well didn't mean everyone had to be miserable.

"Doctor?" Buck was talking to her.

"I'm sorry, what?" she asked.

"Are you ready? Two minutes and counting," he said. "Nobody leaves and nobody new will be allowed to enter the wing. No exceptions. My people are heading over now to lock and guard the door."

"Yes, it's time," Kat said, "no exceptions, Buck. Thank you."

As she started to walk towards the patient wing, she heard the sliding door open behind her. There was a flurry of raised voices as security guards tried to stop someone from entering.

"Sir, sir," the guard said, "you shouldn't go in, sir."

"I'll just be a minute," the voice insisted, "I have to return something."

Kat knew that deep voice and it stopped her in her tracks. It also, in spite of the good sense God gave her, sent a chill of anticipation up her spine.

"I won't bother you, Kat, but I have your phone." She heard Gunnar growl behind her. When she turned, there he was with those same deep blue eyes, hat and boots. And in his hands—those rough cowboy hands—he held out her phone.

"Gunnar," Kat said as she turned to face him. She felt at a loss for words as she reached out in slow motion to retrieve her phone from his outstretched hand.

She could see behind his back that the security guards had closed the sliding doors. Two sentinels on either side stood blocking any exit. Outside, in the driveway by the door, a security car turned its flashers on, dissuading anyone from attempting to enter.

"Gunnar," Kat said again, her face reflecting the emergency flashers from the outside cars. "You have no idea what you've just done."

CHAPTER 9

"Would you look at this quilted mouse, Junie? Looks like a little nurse."

June looked and giggled, while unpacking a pillow made from a flour sack print.

She and her friend, Marta, sat on the floor of the gift shop near the hospital lobby. It was later than they usually locked up. Thanks to an unexpected delivery, they declared it an impromptu inventory night. They'd order a pizza and price the new items.

"Might as well," they agreed, as the men were trout fishing in the river tonight.

"If I ever get sick, Marta," June was saying, "you can cheer me up with anything from this shop—anything at all."

Marta smiled at her friend.

They met years ago, working for a small catering company in town that cooked fancy foods for weddings. Before long, Marta and her husband, Nels, were regulars at church with June and her husband. The four went to lunch every Sunday and played cards once a month.

When the caterers retired and closed their doors, Marta was hired to run the gift shop at the new hospital, and in turn, hired June to help her.

During the week, they delivered meals together to elderly church members, or to new mothers. "Whoever the Holy Spirit tells us to bring a casserole to," they liked to say.

"I couldn't bear to see you sick, Junie," Marta said. "Don't say such things."

But June was distracted. Gazing into the lobby, she saw a teenage boy walk by carrying the same yellow flowers she thought they sold earlier to a woman visiting her mother. June remembered the woman's eyes welling up as she looked at the bouquet, and again while writing out a little card that would stick out of the top.

June felt such compassion for the woman and offered her a box of tissues.

Also, there seemed to be more activity in the hospital in general. West Gorge was growing, it was true. The church was building a larger sanctuary and a gym for the youth group. Down the street, a second elementary school was going up. Even so, theirs was still considered a small community. Yet, she heard and saw more people coming into the medical center this one evening than they usually saw in a week.

"Something's going on, Marta," June said, "and I don't like it."

Marta stopped what she was doing and looked up at her friend. She knew by now that June's instincts were worth heeding. Hadn't she known to take dinner to the widower, Deacon Wendt, when he wasn't even sick—only to find him in his garden, suffering from a stroke? Their early intervention saved him from a much worse outcome.

And June had predicted that the caterers were getting ready to close shop. Marta didn't believe her at first, thinking they'd be around for years. But June had been right.

Silently, they set the gifts down and gazed through the window to the lobby. They saw emergency flashers outside the double sliding doors, and security guards in a huddle.

Standing in the middle of the lobby, Marta and June spotted that nice new doctor, Kat Tate. She was dressed a little strangely for work,

Marta mentioned. *Saucy* is the word that came to June's mind, as she thought of the Bible story about Jezebel.

"Is that a dress she's wearing?" June asked, quietly.

"I reckon," Marta said. "It's not much bigger than one of Nels' compression socks."

"Looks like someone else was going fishing tonight," June said.

Marta smiled and nodded, and the two women watched Doctor Tate, now in a heated discussion with a tall, handsome cowboy. They couldn't make out the words through the window, but the body language was riveting.

"I think that's the oldest West boy," Marta said.

"Oh, I'd say that's a *man,* not a boy," June said.

The doctor had her eyes locked with the cowboy, and Marta would be willing to swear on a stack of Bibles, if anyone asked her, that sparks were flying.

The cowboy was mighty angry at the little doctor, they could see. But she wasn't backing down. With her hands on her hips, standing a full head lower than him in her unsteady heels, she held his gaze without cowering.

This was better than the Hallmark Channel, one whispered to the other.

"Just kiss her, why don'tcha?" Marta said, under her breath.

CHAPTER 10

"*W*hat do you mean, *I can't leave?*" Gunnar said, his voice escalating. "*Of course* I can leave—I only came to drop off your phone!"

"Gunnar..." Kat tried to find the words.

Out of the corner of her eye, she could see the security guard watching them warily.

Kat gave the guard a slight shake of her head, and turned to the cowboy.

"Gunnar, this part of the hospital has been quarantined, I'm afraid, for about a week," she said. "I can't let you go because that would violate the guidelines we just put in place. You could compromise the health of the community."

"You have to be joking, Kat," he yelled. And then added, "is this because of our rotten date—are you punishing me for that? Because let me tell you..."

"Stop!" Kat said, "just stop."

Kat told him to sit down in the lobby while she gathered the others. She wasn't about to have thirty separate conversations like this one. Josh Quell walked in, looking anxious.

"Doctor," he said, "people are asking a lot of questions."

"Okay, okay," she said, fearing it was going to get out of control quickly. "Gather everyone you can, Doctor Quell, and bring them to the lobby—stat."

She looked over and saw Gunnar pacing back and forth, up and down the length of the lobby. He looked like a wild horse that hadn't been broken. Gunnar was an imposing figure of a man. He was tall, and appeared even taller with his boots and hat. And he was strong; she felt his strength firsthand when he unceremoniously tossed her into his truck.

Was that just tonight? With all that had transpired, it felt so long ago.

Back and forth and back and forth, Gunnar pawed the floor with his heavy cowboy boots, digging in his heels with each heavy step. His broad shoulders and muscular arms flexed as his fists clenched and unclenched.

Kat did not think this was going well.

The world of quarantines was not new to Kat—quarantines were an inevitable part of the medical specialty that she chose to study. Viruses had to be isolated in order to contain their spread, but people did not ever like being told where they could or could not go.

With most people, their sense of reason would eventually prevail, but it was a process. And apparently, Gunnar West was going to have trouble processing.

Neanderthal, Kat said under her breath and walked towards him.

"Gunnar…" she said, but he continued to pace like a toddler having a tantrum.

"Gunnar, please stop for a minute," she said. He paused, but then thought the better of it and stomped his boots into the floor while shaking his head.

"Listen to me!" Kat's voice was urgent, but instead of getting louder, it became softer and gentler than it had been moments ago. Maybe that's what got his attention.

He stood still and Kat slowly moved to stand in front of him. The hot breath coming out of his nose and mouth were evidence of his rage and anger. It reminded her of a bull in a pen, about to charge. But he seemed to be trying to control himself.

"The last thing I need, Gunnar West," she said quietly, as the lobby filled up with people, "is a big raging bull in my hospital. Not when I need to deliver bad news to a crowd and establish order."

Gunnar stared at her in anger. When he did speak, he was also quiet.

"*Your* hospital? Let me give you a news flash, Kat Tate," he said, "this is *my* hospital. My family donated it to the town—which bears my name. My name is also on this building. I sit on the board. And I don't like being told I can't leave *my* hospital, in *my* town, when I want to. Especially by a woman who, apparently, can only hold onto a man if she locks him up!"

His words shocked Kat and hurt her deeply. Gunnar could see the confusion in her eyes. It may have satisfied him for a moment, but Kat rebounded quickly.

"Well you may own the town. And you may own the West Gorge Medical Center, cowboy," she said. "But right now, I am the *sheriff*."

CHAPTER 11

*I*t was a shootout and Kat won, but she felt wounded.

Gunnar had aimed right for the heart and didn't miss. Kat could see he was still fighting mad about being stuck in the hospital. Maybe he'd never been in a situation that his stature or his name couldn't get him out of, Kat thought.

She had to push back, though, and let him know that while his name might be on the building, she was the one in charge.

"Everybody, please be seated and quiet down," Kat told the crowd in the lobby. "I will answer all your questions as best I can. Sit down, please." Thirty or so people created a steady buzz with their talking, and the volume was increasing. They wanted answers, she knew, but they also wanted to be heard.

Kat was not accustomed to the crowd control aspect of a quarantine. Until now, her place had been a row or two back from the director in charge. Over time, with knowledge and seniority, she was positioned closer to the patients, family and the press.

Today, Kat was front and center.

Refusing to allow the escalating tempers to control the room, she spoke.

"The longer y'all take to quiet down," Kat said in her no-nonsense voice, "the more our patients will have to wait for the care they need. Many of them are your loved ones."

People quieted immediately.

"Now then," she spoke. "I am Doctor Tate, and this is my chief intern, Doctor Quell."

Josh stood next to Kat and nodded.

"We are infectious disease specialists," she said, letting this statement sink in. "For the past few days, we've had folks coming in with severe flu symptoms and respiratory distress. It's actually a dangerous virus that's spreading, and much more serious than the common flu."

Kat went on to tell the assembled group that they would all be quarantined in the wing of the hospital for approximately a week. The good news, she told them, was that the incubation period was short, as was the duration of the contagion.

"The virus is called ResVi for short," she said. "It attacks quickly and is extremely contagious. It can be deadly. Those with pre-existing conditions such as asthma, COPD, and auto-immune diseases are susceptible and at risk for severe reactions."

She gave everyone a moment to gasp and turn to each other.

"By containing the virus here, we can slow or stop the spread to our community. That means fewer deaths, miscarriages, seizures and dangerously high fevers," Kat said. "Are you beginning to understand how critical this quarantine is?"

There were murmurs and a few grudging nods. Kat looked over at Gunnar, but his face was not any softer than when they spoke minutes ago.

"Now," she went on, "some of you are going to fall ill, and there's no better place to be than right here. West Gorge Medical Center is new, well-staffed and equipped to take care of you. In the meantime, we will see to your food and lodging. If you need medications or a favorite book, call home and request a small suitcase be dropped off at the security check point."

She looked around at the shocked and nervous faces of people responding to her clinical tones, and suddenly felt great compassion for everyone.

"Look," Kat said to the gathered audience, softening her voice. "I understand that you are all inconvenienced, frightened, and a little bit angry. I know what I'm asking sounds crazy and over the top."

The group nodded in agreement.

"But I'm asking you to please trust the hospital—trust me—in this decision."

Many of the faces looking back at her seemed to soften as she spoke, but she avoided glancing at Gunnar.

"The quarantine should only be a week. It will pass quickly if we work together. And by staying in place," she said, "by staying here and reading books and watching TV for a few days, we can avoid taking this potentially devastating illness to our families, our stores, our schools, our churches and our neighbors."

This had been the right approach. Kat could see shoulders and faces relax.

She then mobilized the nurses and medical assistants to begin gathering names and medical information for those who would be staying. The staff would point every person to a bed and give them a set of scrubs to change into if they wanted.

"One last thing," Kat said, before the group dispersed, "this is not a hotel and my staff is not here to serve you. There will be a commissary set up in the break room for simple meals, and everybody cleans up after themselves, *Capiche?*"

"Yes, Doctor Tate," said a chorus of lackluster guests... hostages... Kat wasn't sure.

"We will reconvene tomorrow morning for an update," Josh Quell told them all.

As Kat began walking over towards Gunnar to check in with him, she spotted a young teenage boy heading her way. It was the same boy she noticed earlier, still holding the bouquet of flowers. He seemed unaware of Gunnar's presence nearby.

"Doc!" he implored with big doe eyes, "you *gotta* let me out of here. I can't stay."

The kid looked like he was 12 but sounded older—maybe 14 or 15.

"You can't leave, nobody can," she said. "But who are you visiting and why are you here so late—shouldn't you be home in bed?"

At being told he couldn't leave, the boy's pretend innocence was replaced by a belligerent sneer as his gaze wandered up and down from Kat's cleavage to her legs.

"Shouldn't *you* be home in bed?" he said.

Kat's mouth fell open in shock, but before she could reprimand the boy, Gunnar took two huge strides and placed his strong hands on the boy's shoulders, holding him in place.

"What the..." the boy writhed in alarm against Gunnar's restraint.

"You owe the lady an apology," Gunnar growled.

"Uh... *hey*, you're hurting me, man," the kid whined.

Gunnar didn't budge, and neither did Kat. It would be good to establish a few ground rules.

"I said," Gunnar repeated, "apologize to the lady. Now."

"Okay, okay," the boy said, "I was out of line and I'm sorry. Now *let go!*"

Gunnar released the boy and Kat was about to ask him again who he was visiting, when a woman came over to the trio. "There they are. I brought those very same flowers to mother this afternoon and they disappeared—look, they still have my little card attached," she said.

All eyes turned to the boy. The security guard, who was listening, walked a little closer to the group. A man walked over and said, "hey officer, my gold wristwatch disappeared! I took it off in the washroom to scrub my hands, and it's gone."

The boy looked like a frightened rabbit, Kat could see. She was beginning to feel sorry for him when she looked down at a glint of stainless steel in the pocket of his coat.

"May I?" she asked him.

He looked around him and saw the security guard, the cowboy, the doctor, the man with the missing watch, and the woman who brought flowers to her mother, then reluctantly nodded. Kat reached over and pulled her very own stethoscope from his pocket. He must have lifted it from behind the nurses' station where she left it earlier. This one had her name engraved. It was a graduation gift from her mom.

"Look, I'm sorry," he said feebly, shoulders sagging. Then he handed the flowers back to the rightful giver and dropped his head in defeat.

"Why, you little thief. What else have you got in those oversized pockets?" Gunnar asked.

The boy, who said his name was Ash Gibson, pulled out a man's gold wristwatch, two cell phones, a candy bar and $47.50 in cash.

CHAPTER 12

*Y*ou owe the lady an apology.

Gunnar's words played through Kat's mind as she gathered her rag-tag staff in the lobby very late that night. He referred to her as a "lady," which was surprising, considering how he treated her earlier in the evening.

Still, the rough and tough cowboy had come to her defense against the young criminal tonight, and Kat had to admit it felt good. A man had been there when she needed him, which was a new sensation, given that her own father was absent during her high school years.

She could have used a protector and defender. Someone to tell teenage boys to have more respect than honking the car when they picked her up. Someone to say, "have her home by ten," even though Kat would protest and fuss at him, she'd know it was because he cared.

Kat was impressed that the cowboy set his strong feelings aside to right a wrong on her behalf, even though he was frustrated with her and the quarantine. And even though she hadn't been particularly kind to him on their date.

· · ·

"FIND THE COMMON THREAD," KAT TOLD HER STAFF IN THEIR BRIEF lobby meeting, suppressing a yawn. She gave them their marching orders before they dispersed. "How did the ResVi get here? Where have all these people been, and where is it heading?"

Josh Quell had been on the phone with the CDC and they wanted answers, too. Epidemics like this one didn't appear out of nowhere. They had an origin and a swath of devastation.

Kat was also busy holding the hand of Shep Arndt, who'd never approved a hospital shut-down in his long career and was second guessing the extremes they'd gone to. Shep had to answer to his board of directors, his employees and the community.

"Look, Shep," Kat had told him, "people aren't coming to Wyoming on covered wagons anymore. You've got major airports, big cities and tour buses by the score. Visitors from every continent are inundating your natural wonders and gift shops, and it's a double-edged sword. You boost the economy, but you also increase Wyoming's exposure to all sorts of nasty things."

"I know," Shep sighed. "That's why we brought you on—in the nick of time, it seems."

"I'm not happy about the virus," Kat told him, "but I'm glad to be here."

LIKE KAT, JOSH HAD BEEN ON HIS FEET SINCE EARLY MORNING. AT nearly two in the morning, all seemed quiet. Kat and Josh were the only two remaining in the lobby following the staff meeting.

"I just realized how tired I am," Kat told Josh, "and you must be too."

"Yes, but I'll mind the store for a little longer while you get some sleep, Kat."

"I'm going to find an empty bed and do just that," she said. "Then I'll spell you."

Josh smiled and pointed a tired hand at her mid-section.

"I suggest you peel off that candy wrapper and put on scrubs, first."

For a moment, his comment didn't register. She had been too busy to realize she still wore the little dress, and the heels to go with it.

"Oh my gosh," Kat said with a loud laugh, thinking back to her ill-fated date with the cowboy, the big lummox who appeared not to know how to act in a nice restaurant. She didn't bother lowering her voice when she exclaimed, "a few hours ago, I thought my night couldn't get any worse. Boy was I wrong."

Finishing her statement, Kat pivoted towards the linen room and smacked squarely into Gunnar West.

"Whoa, excuse me!" she said. He instinctively reached out and put both arms fully around her waist to steady her, then pulled her close. She would have toppled over otherwise.

He didn't let go and Kat didn't pull away.

Instead, she breathed in and savored the comfort of him for a moment. Whatever else he *wasn't*, he was substantial and rugged, and very good looking. Glancing into his deep blue eyes, she regretted her unkind words, which he surely must have heard.

Neither one moved.

Standing close together in an unexpected embrace, Kat said, "I was just going to…"

She couldn't string together the words.

"To…?" Gunnar asked, softly. The low rumble of his voice sent a tremor through her.

"To change…" she said at last, "into something more comfortable."

"That's a nice way to end a date," Gunnar said playfully. The slight smirk softened his features. It would be so easy to smile back, Kat thought, but then remembered the many ways he had insulted her that night.

"Oh, our date ended long ago, Gunnar," Kat said icily, forgetting his chivalry, and focusing instead on the humiliation she felt earlier. "Probably when you tossed me into your truck like a bale of hay."

The smile faded from Gunnar's face as he dropped his arms, causing the doctor to step back hard and regain her balance. Kat silently kicked herself, wishing she hadn't said anything. His arms had felt very nice. Even though they were his arms, they were warm and solid as tree limbs. It had been a very long time since she felt so secure and cared for. For a moment, Kat could believe everything was going to be okay.

"That's funny," Gunnar said, anger flashing once again, "throwing you into my truck was the highlight of the night for me. Second only to throwing you out."

He turned and stomped off in the other direction.

While Kat stood with her mouth open, incensed at Gunnar's unkindness, she was vaguely aware of Josh Quell behind her in the lobby, making a whistling noise like the dropping of an atomic bomb.

CHAPTER 13

*M*aybe *I was too hard on the girl.*
Prior to smacking head-on into Kat Tate, Gunnar decided he might have been too critical of the doctor, even though she trapped him in a situation he found unbearable.

As a man, he felt unsettled and angry with her, and the embers smoldered. But as a board member of the hospital, he was quite impressed with the way she took charge of the quarantined group.

Even in her little blue dress, she had a natural authority—Kat didn't yell to communicate that her words were important, and that got Gunnar's attention more than anything.

On the ranch, he found that a cool head always prevailed. While other cowboys and ranch hands sometimes liked to shout, Gunnar learned from his father that a calm voice was much more effective when it came to steadying unbroken fillies, especially when the horses' every instinct told them to buck, rear up and pull away.

"Why, shoot!" Gunnar said out loud, as he recalled his and Kat's heated conversation in the lobby, realizing it was the same calm voice she used on him when he was bucking up and pulling away.

Gunnar was embarrassed, but had to smile.

Respect to the sheriff.

He had been circling back to offer an olive branch when she plowed into him at full speed, while loudly bashing him and their disastrous date to Doctor Quell; telling Josh what a rotten night it had been.

Hearing her words made Gunnar start to lose his precarious sense of good will, but when Kat crashed right into his chest, he was conflicted. His arms weren't conflicted though—they instinctively wrapped around her and she didn't pull away.

While she was close and in his arms, he had to admit she felt nice. She smelled nice. And contrary to his first impression, she looked very nice—beautiful, in fact. Whether or not he approved of her choice of first-date attire was beside the point. She made an effort.

Gunnar thought back to a few hours before, and realized he might have made more of an effort himself. He didn't need to pick up a lady in his tall truck. What was he thinking? He should have anticipated that she'd be wearing a dress and would find it hard to get in the front seat. He had a fleet of vehicles to choose from, including a sports car and a sedan, even a Jeep. Any car would have been a more considerate choice.

And just because he was used to wearing his cowboy hat and jeans every day at the ranch didn't mean he had to go full western on his date with the doctor. He had an MBA, for crying out loud. He owned and managed one of the largest cattle ranches in the state. He sat on multiple boards. He invested in small businesses and mentored high school students interested in business and ranching. Yet, tonight he presented himself like a clumsy oaf who didn't know how to order a bottle of wine in a nice restaurant.

Gunnar was ashamed of his behavior and knew that as much as he wanted to give Jackie a hard time, it was he who was going to get an earful from her—and it would be deserved. He would take it like a man.

He should not have stomped away the way he did just now, while trying to make amends. Too easily, he let Kat's words set him off. What was it about this girl that brought out the worst in him? Kat knew he didn't throw her out of his truck, but the hurt look on her face was almost worth the fib. That is, until his mother's face came into his mind and he thought of how disappointed she would be.

"You can be a cowboy *and* a gentleman, Gunnar," she told him many times.

Gunnar could not win tonight. He had stirred up and angered the hornet's nest and now he was trapped with it for a week. Someone was bound to get stung.

Kat had too much on her mind to be worried about Gunnar West. She had sick patients and angry people under quarantine. Her director, Shep Arndt, was questioning her judgment—even if he didn't come right out and say so. The PR team wanted a statement to give to the press about the virus. The CDC wanted to know what her team had discovered about the origin, so they could track the travel pattern and the spread of the virus.

All Kat wanted was a few hours' sleep.

But Gunnar's words played through her mind as she closed her eyes. He told her, yelled at her, that a quarantine was the only way she could hold onto a man. As if Gunnar West was a man she wanted to hold onto under any circumstances. Then he said how good it felt to throw her out of his truck. That hurt her feelings, even if it wasn't true.

If Kat was a crier, this would be a good time to shed a few tears to help her drift off to sleep. But she did not cry easily. Instead, she got quieter and quieter as she internalized, and tried to make sense of hurts and slights.

It's how she got through her parents' divorce and her father's abandonment.

It's how she got through countless lonely college nights when she stayed in to study, while her friends went to parties. And why not? Her friends chose career paths that came to a hard stop at job offers after four years—jobs in marketing, sales and engineering.

All perfectly fine careers, but not ones Kat aspired to.

While her friends graduated and took trips, fell in love and planned each other's weddings, Kat Tate studied on in resigned solitude, until she was the last friend standing. It hurt Kat that nobody asked her to be a bridesmaid, but she understood. She barely had time to attend the weddings themselves, let alone all the showers and parties.

At least they remembered to invite her to the big day.

And whoever planned the seating chart was thrilled, no doubt, to get her RSVP card and have a single guest to stick anywhere they needed. Often, to round out a table of misfits.

"One chicken, please," she'd say.

So far, Kat had been placed by a 13-year-old nephew who kept dropping his roll to look at her bare legs, a grandmother on oxygen, (check the tube for kinks Kat, if you don't mind), and cousins from Poland who spoke no English. She'd sat at the kiddie table, next to frisky widowers, and, one time, with all the single aunts, from both sides of the aisle.

Still, she soldiered on. Kat stayed focused on medical school, then her internship, and finally, a placement at the Chicago hospital—at the exclusion of all else. But these accomplishments didn't keep her warm at night, or protect her from the pain of being left out.

"Always a doctor and never a bride," a friend had jabbed at the most recent wedding she attended—alone. The wedding where she wore the dress she had on tonight. Admittedly, it was the shortest and most revealing of all her guest dresses.

Kat was embarrassed now at how transparent her loneliness must be to others—showing up for wedding after wedding without a date, wearing one dress after another that screamed "look at me, not the happy couple."

As if a stretchy tube of rouched fabric could be considered a dress.

She cringed to think she picked this tube of fabric for a first date in her new town. Be honest, Kat, she thought, the first date she'd had in a very, very long time, in any town.

"Stupid girl!" Kat said into her pillow before falling into a deep sleep.

CHAPTER 14

"When was your last physical?"

"Two months ago," Gunnar grumbled.

"Major surgeries?"

"None," he said.

"Have you left the country in the past six months?"

"Nope," he said again.

Gunnar had been sleeping in an empty hospital bed for about five hours when a pretty little nurse came in to get his medical history. He was stretched out with his boots still on, and his cowboy hat over his face to block the lights from the hallway.

Without removing the hat from his face, he turned his head and squinted at her with one eye. She had her hair piled on her head and wore blue scrubs and oversized eyeglasses. She was pretty enough, with her long eyelashes and high cheekbones—that's about all he could see with her head bowed down over a medical chart.

She could very well have nice legs, he thought, if they weren't concealed under the long scrub pants. On her feet, she wore white running shoes with bright pink laces.

No wedding ring, Gunnar noted, while thinking she was probably too young for him. Still, it was nice to look at pretty young girls and maybe flirt a little. Once they found out who he was, they usually started the flirting.

This one seemed to be all business.

Turning his head back under his hat, Gunnar closed his eyes and answered her rapid-fire questions, not hiding the impatience in his voice. He hoped to get a bit more sleep.

"Are you up-to-date on your inoculations?"

"Yep," he said.

"Tetanus shot?"

"Yep," he said.

"Last flu shot?"

"November," he said.

"Any asthma, or COPD?"

"Nope," he sighed.

"How about family history," she said, "are your parents both living?"

Gunnar was quiet for a moment before answering.

"My father is living," he said with a gruff voice.

The nurse was also quiet for a minute before continuing.

"Do you have a family history of diabetes, heart disease or cancer?"

Gunnar exhaled audibly before answering. As he spoke, there was a slight but unmistakable quaver in his voice.

"My mother... she died of breast cancer. Three years ago," he said.

After a longer pause than Gunnar would have expected from a young nurse who didn't know him from a hole in the ground, she answered with a great deal of warmth in her voice.

"Gunnar... I'm so sorry to hear that," she said. "That must have been painful for you and for your family. My sincere condolences."

With that change in tone, Gunnar thought he recognized the voice but couldn't place it, or reconcile it with his quick glance at the nurse's face. Maybe she was an acquaintance from church, or the town. He'd grown up in West Gorge—she could be anyone.

Gunnar sat up.

Swinging his legs over the side, he removed his hat and placed it on the bed.

Taking a closer look at the compassionate eyes and face looking back at him, he saw that it wasn't a nurse at all, but Doctor Kat Tate, looking for all the world like a different person in her scrubs, with her hair pulled away from her face.

Her makeup was gone and she wore a light gloss on her lips.

"Is that you, Kat?" he asked.

"Yep," Kat said. "I'm helping the nursing staff gather medical histories. The CDC is breathing down my neck for data. Sorry I had to wake you."

Gunnar was speechless.

"One more thing," Kat said. "I have to get a temperature reading. The virus is only contagious with a fever, and that's the first symptom."

As he opened his mouth to protest that he felt just fine, she stuck a basal thermometer under his tongue and instructed him to clamp down and hold it. Meanwhile, she put her stethoscope on her ears and placed the bell on his chest and heart.

She was so close and so still that it made him nervous. Though why, he didn't know.

He could smell her clean skin with every breath. He found his arms wanting to reach up and encircle her waist, just as he had the night before in the lobby, when she bumped into him.

Gunnar tried to look off into space, but couldn't stop himself from gazing into her eyes—bright green, like a meadow in Spring. He hadn't noticed. Without the makeup, her scrubbed skin was a beautiful complexion that reminded him of the bushel of ripe peaches Justice bought every August for pies and jam.

He could feel his pulse quickening and tried to breath steadily to calm it down.

"Your heartrate is a slightly elevated," she told him as she pulled away. And was it his imagination, or was Kat smirking just a bit when she said this?

After she wrote a few things on his chart, she made a parting comment, then left.

"Don't worry, cowboy," she said, "you're not hot."

CHAPTER 15

"Well, you all survived the first night?"

Except for the sick patients, the quarantined group was gathered again in the hospital lobby for an update and Kat took center stage. Coffee and donuts had been delivered to the break room along with breakfast sandwiches and fruit. Most everyone had something in their hand, and many wore loaner hospital scrubs.

"You look like my medical school classmates," she joked, and was rewarded with a light round of laughter. Even Gunnar managed to smile a bit, though he had the same clothes on as the day before.

Also standing near the back was young Ash, who was eyeing a woman's open purse.

"First order of business, place your valuables in the break room lockers—I'd hate to see anything get lost or stolen," Kat announced, making sure to catch Ash's eyes as she said this. In turn, he looked at her with feigned innocence and shrugged.

Gunnar couldn't take his eyes off of Kat and continued to marvel at the transformation. What if she had been waiting for him last night wearing running shoes and scrubs? He almost wished she had—but no. In spite of the epic failure of Kat's dress and heels, he liked that she had taken the time to dress for him and wished he'd done the same for her.

But he liked this new, confident Kat Tate, and he wanted to clear the air. Though it didn't take a genius to understand that this was not the time or the place. As the hospital's leading authority on infectious diseases—in the middle of its first epidemic—Kat was the center of attention.

With her messy hair bun, wide-framed glasses and jogging shoes, and without cosmetics, Doctor Kat Tate was the prettiest girl at the dance right now.

And he couldn't take his eyes off of her.

"A tour bus with overseas travelers," she said, "apparently stopped at Cindy's Roadside Diner up by the freeway for lunch four days ago."

Several people nodded. For though it was 20 miles away, it was a popular stop for West Gorge residents heading to some of the big box stores to stock up on groceries and supplies.

"At least two people on the bus who ate at Cindy's tested positive for the virus the next day at an urgent care facility two hundred miles from here, where they presented fevers and body aches," Kat said. "Sadly, the test results for the virus were not confirmed until after the bus with the other exposed people left for the next town."

Everyone collectively groaned.

"Those with the virus ate at Cindy's salad bar," Kat said, "and proceeded to contaminate a string of restaurants, hotels and tourist attractions over the past few days. And now," she waited until she had everyone's full attention, "nearly everyone on the bus is hospitalized, with three in critical condition."

There was silence as people let that sink in.

"The state and CDC have closed down a dozen attractions and restaurants for disinfecting, including Cindy's Diner," Kat said, "resulting in thousands of lost dollars for Cindy and lost wages for her staff."

Gunnar frowned at this news. Cindy was a friend of his father, and Ridge would be distressed to hear of her misfortune. They also knew some of the waitresses, including a few who could not last very long without their income and tips. He'd send an email to the foundation to see if they could route some emergency funds to help them out.

"I know from experience that there will be dozens of people who have come into contact with these tourists," Kat said, "who are now contagious themselves without knowing it, or who are sick without knowing why. They will be showing up at hospitals very soon, and those hospitals will also have to make tough decisions about whether to quarantine. Unless the CDC makes the decision for them."

"It's like a wildfire," someone in the front row of seats said and everyone agreed.

"That's a good way of looking at it," Kat said. "While we can't put out all the big and little fires burning throughout the state, we can work together to keep as many in our community as safe as possible, and from getting burned."

At that, the crowd nodded.

Kat closed her medical chart and tucked her pen back in her pocket, then nodded at Josh. It was time to make rounds of all those infected—the number was now up to 18. That was nearly one third of everyone being isolated. They'd have to bring in a few more doctors and nurses.

She'd call Shep.

KAT, JOSH, AND THE MEDICAL TEAM DIVIDED THE HOSPITAL AREAS INTO A ward for the sick, rooms for those who had been exposed or who were at high risk, and those with the greatest chance of skipping the virus altogether.

The good news was that people were only contagious when they had a fever, and generally, the fever only lasted two or three days. The other good news was that the incubation period was short. Once exposed, if someone didn't become feverish in two days, they were likely immune. This is why Kat was comfortable saying the quarantine period could be as short as one week.

She could only hope she or Josh would not get sick. Unlike at the bigger hospitals, they didn't have a large staff backing them up.

CHAPTER 16

*G*unnar West had never called in sick a day in his life. Not to school as a boy, or to work as a man. Although, as a kid he sometimes wished he could just stay home even one day and play video games, or maybe sleep in a little later than his morning chores dictated.

"Should I go tell the livestock that their breakfast will have to wait, Gunnar, so you can get a little more shuteye—a little more *beauty rest?*" Ridge had half-jokingly asked him once when he was an adolescent, complaining about rising so early every morning.

They only had that conversation one time, for to push Ridge West to a point where his good-natured digs had to become serious reprimands was something Gunnar had never been willing to do. He understood that the West name, and the West fortune, came with benefits and therefore obligations.

First of all, his younger brothers watched him like hawks and copied his every move. That alone was a huge responsibility. Gunnar understood that if he was disrespectful to Ridge or Randi, Pike and Colton might feel free to act the same.

They watched his every move, even now.

He knew the bar was set pretty high for the family and that they had to set an example for everyone on the ranch to follow.

Gunnar knew that some days, a ranch hand came to work with a cold or a flu and pushed through for the sake of feeding their families. Of course, the Wests wouldn't expect them to keep working, and would never let anyone go hungry, or without basic necessities.

But there was an invisible code whereby a cowboy had to pull his own weight. Ridge rarely interfered.

A time or two, Gunnar could recall Ridge or their ranch foreman laying a hand on a cowboy and quietly telling him to hit the bunkhouse for a bit. And now that Gunnar was manager of the ranch, he knew firsthand that no paychecks were ever docked for sick time.

Still, he was glad not to be bringing the virus back to West Ranch and exposing his aging father and old Justice, or the rest of their hard-working staff. Even if it meant that Pike and Colton would have to step up and cover Gunnar's responsibilities for the week.

"Are there any pretty girls in town crying over your quarantine?" Pike asked him on the phone. "I'd be glad to pay them a visit on your behalf brother, and dry their tears."

"Nope," he told Pike, thinking of how the well had run dry for him in West Gorge, but hoped that wasn't true for his brothers. The West men couldn't all stay bachelors for the rest of their lives, could they? "No girls. No tears," he said. And then thought of the pretty doctor with the sparks in her eyes. Gunnar had said hurtful things to her, he knew; things he wasn't proud of. She had every right to cry, yet had stood up to him and given it right back.

Pike was just elbowing him in the ribs, he knew. Probably to bring some humor to the situation. His brother surely knew that of all places to be locked in, the West Gorge Medical Center was the last place Gunnar would want to be. The eldest of the brothers stated more than once that he would gladly heal his own wounds and cure his own fevers before willingly visit that hospital.

But he'd never had to put his money where his mouth was.

Gunnar's parents used to joke that the boys inherited their "healthy pioneer stock," as they were a uniquely strong and robust family. It was easy for the boys to start believing that illness was a sign of weakness, and that the Wests stayed in top health because they worked hard and made good choices.

That is, until Randi West discovered a mass in her breast during a routine exam. That's when the dam broke loose at West Ranch. And it didn't have a happy ending.

Ridge pined for his beloved Randi every day, and Gunnar and his brothers did too. She was the heart and soul of the ranch and surrounding community. So many were touched by her kindness that the funeral chapel overflowed with mourners.

Just about every teacher in West Gorge showed up, thankful for the beautiful schools Randi insisted the town should have—and the librarians, thankful for the countless shelves of books donated by Randi. Young mothers came in droves, each the recipient of thoughtful gifts of diapers, blankets and other necessities.

Randi single handedly, through the foundation and her personal account, kept local businesses thriving. She was a faithful customer of Painted Bird art gallery, the West Gorge Spa, and the town outfitters, just to name a few local establishments.

"My dear friend Randi painted this town with generosity, using both a wide brush and delicate, detailed strokes," Jackie's mother eloquently said in her eulogy of Randi.

If Randi were alive today, Gunnar was sure she would be on the phone to Cindy from the diner, asking how she could help. She would personally send gift cards and money to Cindy's waitresses to help them through the forced shut-down. Randi would also be sending notes and gifts to the overworked hospital staff during the epidemic, and providing special meals and treats to keep their spirits up.

Aside from the West family, this was his mother's legacy.

She was proud of her accomplishments as a corporate attorney, but her passion was for diving right in and helping people. Working alongside Ridge at the ranch, and at the West Foundation, she had abundant opportunities to live her best life, helping others live theirs.

Even at the end, although Gunnar hated to think about those days, she was more concerned about her husband and boys, and even the hospital staff, than herself. Yet, Gunnar rebelled against the hospital and avoided it when possible. Except for the quarterly board meetings, he tried not to step foot inside. The soothing colors of the walls, the living vegetation wall, the classical music—they all irritated him and reminded him of his saddest days.

He was already angry and stomping like a wild stallion at having to walk inside to bring Kat her missing phone. But when she told him he couldn't leave, he felt trapped and out of control. All he could see was his mother's ravaged face; her beautiful hair gone but for a few precious strands.

Once again, he thought of his wonderful mother, and how she would be looking at him if she were here. It would be a subtle glance, but one that would communicate how much more she expected of him, but loved him all the same.

"Stop pacing the lobby like a wild mustang Gunnar," she would say with a smile. "You're frightening the poor lil' doctor, who is only trying to do her job."

CHAPTER 17

at had many jobs during an epidemic and wore different hats. She was the medical specialist and the voice of reason. If she made a blunder, she'd be the scapegoat for Shep Arndt and the hospital board.

She was the contact for the CDC.

If the PR team had their way, she would be the press liaison.

Within the hospital walls she was healer, leader, and calmer of anxieties. She was the organizer, the hostess of the break room, and the cruise director.

In one of the shared rooms, she had been the fixer of the remote control, and the finder of the home network for a group of gals who turned the quarantine into a craft retreat.

"Out of the ashes of tragedy," Kat said quietly to herself, "comes a scrapbook."

But one thing she refused to be was babysitter to a big angry cowboy who couldn't control his temper when the doors closed him in, and pouted when he had to wake up and give his medical history.

Kat was deeply sorry that he lost his mother to such a harsh disease, but loss was part of life. At least, it had been part of hers.

And she had news for him and everyone else here: people do not come to hospitals to sleep, or sleep in. They were awakened according to nursing shifts and doctor rounds. At the discretion and convenience of the staff, not the other way around.

This was not a spa or a vacation.

And just as she had gotten herself worked up thinking about these things, Kat rounded the corner into a break room that was otherwise empty except for young Ash, who was rifling through a wallet and pulling out a few twenties.

"Is that your wallet, Ash?" Kat asked him, causing him to jump.

"What?... Oh…yeah," he fumbled.

Kat took the wallet from the stunned boy and opened it up.

"You must have lost a few pounds, Ash," she said, looking at the license. "Or should I call you Glen Green, an overweight fifty-year-old man with cataracts?"

Ash let his shoulders drop.

"Ash, listen," Kat said, "I'm sure that in spite of your poor life decisions, you're a good kid. But I do not have time to rehabilitate you. And while I'd like to lock you in the storage closet for a week, I fear you'd steal all our toilet paper. Come with me."

As he worked to keep up with a very purposeful Kat—she was much faster in her runners than in her heels—she asked him what his parents would say when they came to fetch him and learned about the trouble he'd gotten into.

"My parents are long gone," he said, and Kat slowed her pace. "I live with my granny."

Ash went on to tell her that his parents dropped him off with his grandmother for a few days and never returned. That was four years ago, when he was eleven. They sent him a card every now and then from Mexico with a few dollars in it.

"Granny isn't doing so good, that's why I need to get out of here," he said. "She sometimes forgets what day it is. She forgets we need groceries."

A string of lies with a grain of truth? Kat wondered.

She would ask that someone from West Gorge Human Services

make a wellness visit. If Granny has all her faculties, she may be worried about Ash. Or she might be relieved to have Ash out of her house for a few days.

Or... she may not remember him at all.

When she and Ash reached the room where Gunnar had been snoozing, she asked him to wait in the hallway.

"Stay here. Try not to take anything," she told him, and walked into the room, gently closing the door behind her.

Gunnar was sitting in a chair, reading an outdated news magazine.

"Sheriff," he frowned at Kat and nodded.

Kat smiled and said, "I'm glad you remembered."

Gunnar looked up at her.

"Raise your right hand, cowboy," Kat said. "As sheriff, I'm deputizing you."

"Is that right?" he asked, as he put the magazine down and sat a little straighter. Kat hoped he wasn't going to give her trouble because she had enough on her plate.

"That's right, I don't have eyes enough to keep track of the *Artful Dodger,* so I need you to stick like glue to our resident pick pocket," she said.

Lowering her voice to a whisper, Kat quickly gave Gunnar the rundown, repeating the story Ash told her about his absentee parents and senile grandmother. She shrugged to indicate she couldn't vouch for anything the kid said.

"I'll make a few calls," she said, and then she called Ash to come in.

Gunnar looked at Ash warily, sizing him up anew.

"You need a nanny, dude?" Gunnar taunted him.

"I don't need anything, man," Ash answered with a flash of anger.

They were oil and water, Kat could see, but this was the best she could do for now.

"Whatever way you two work this out is fine with me," Kat said. "Father figure and prodigal son, big brother and his little shadow, or new best friends—I truly do not care. Just keep the boy's hands out of the cookie jar, Gunnar."

She left the room, knowing Gunnar and Ash were shooting daggers at each other with their eyes. A few daggers were aimed at her, no doubt.

CHAPTER 18

Gunnar just couldn't seem to get it right. Every time he crossed paths with Kat, it ended badly. When he talked himself into a fresh start with the good doctor, she zinged him. So, his plan was to stay far away from her, but that didn't work either.

Apparently, she was going to hunt him down and then zing him again.

For a hot minute, he was actually happy to see her walk into the hospital room where he sat, until she deputized him of all things.

Saddled him, was more like it. With the bad-mannered thief of a kid. If it was any consolation, the moping kid sitting next to him didn't look like he was thrilled about the arrangement either.

Gunnar wasn't used to being around people who didn't want to be around him—this was a new and unpleasant experience. After all, he grew up in this town; his family had founded and funded the town for generations.

Wherever he went, people waved and smiled at the tall and handsome Gunnar West. Men on the ranch respected him. Women in the town wanted to date him. Teenagers at the school wanted to be mentored by him. But in this group of quarantine castaways, nobody even knew who he was, or they didn't seem to care.

The one pretty woman in the bunch, who he'd actually had a date with, couldn't stand being near him. And the one teenager wanted nothing from him. In his own defense, what could he offer the kid? Ash was more likely to go to jail than go into business if he didn't change his ways. Gunnar realized the kid was saying something.

"Sorry, what?" Gunnar asked.

"I said, what's with the getup, man, the boots and hat... do you work at one of those chuckwagon-themed restaurants?"

Gunnar bristled at the kid's question, thinking what a long week it was going to be.

"I own a ranch outside of town," Gunnar said at last.

"Wow. A real ranch, with *giddy-ups* and *yee haws* and all that?" Ash asked.

"Yup, all those phrases, all the time," Gunnar drawled. "That's just how we talk."

"That's cool," Ash said, "I've never even been close to a horse."

"Well, they're big," Gunnar said. "Hard to steal. Hard to put in your pocket."

"Touché man, you got me where it hurts," Ash said, not sounding hurt at all.

"Hungry?" Gunnar asked, thinking how the walls of the room closed in on him with every word spoken by the kid.

"Yes. Let's go *rustle up* something," Ash said. "Is that how we talk on the ranch?"

Gunnar turned his head to look out the window before reacting, or overreacting. Ash was nothing more than a mustang; a wild young buck. He needed a steady hand and for Gunnar to keep his cool even as every button was being pushed by the kid.

And while it was a drag being with Ash, Gunnar had to admit that the challenge was a more interesting proposition than sitting in a little room reading magazines for a week.

"You got it kid," Gunnar turned and said to Ash with a smile, slapping his hand down hard on Ash's thigh. "Let's go rustle up some grub."

In a silent yell at the cowboy's slap, Ash's mouth shot open in shock and pain. Once he could stand, he limped after Gunnar. Ash silently vowed to be more careful going forward.

KAT STOOD IN THE BREAKROOM, EATING A SANDWICH FROM A TRAY THAT had been delivered by a food service worker in a hazmat suit and gloves. The room had been stocked with microwaveable meals and grab-and-go snacks, sodas, coffee, and a basket of fresh fruit. The best restaurants in town delivered hot meals in the afternoon.

After just two days, the room was starting to look like a frat house kitchen, but it smelled like a hospital, with the liberal use of disinfectant being applied throughout the quarantined wing.

"It burns your nostrils," she said to Gunnar and Ash when they walked into the breakroom wrinkling their noses, "but you get used to it."

"That sandwich probably tastes like pine cleaner," Ash said with distaste.

"My stomach doesn't care," Kat said to the two of them. "When I have more time than this I eat in my secret hiding spot, without the intrusion of disinfectants."

"Where's that?" Ash asked Kat.

"If I told you it wouldn't be a secret," she answered and smiled. "But in the meantime, it's good to know the staff is working hard to keep surfaces free from the germs that can cause the virus to spread."

"I'm not worried," Ash boasted, "it's the old people that catch this, not me."

Kat and Gunnar rolled their eyes.

"Do you ever get time to sit down, Kat?" Gunnar asked her, both of them ignoring the kid's remarks. "You couldn't have gotten more than four hours of sleep last night or the night before. And you're always on the run."

Kat chewed the last bite of her sandwich and wiped the mustard off her chin.

"Ah, the glamorous life of a doctor," she told him. "I won't get a lot of sleep this week, but that's to be expected. When I need to, I'll crash if I can."

Gunnar nodded. His days started early, but with the exception of Spring, when animals on the ranch were giving birth, he could count on getting a full night's rest. His respect for Kat grew a little more, for the stamina she had for her job.

Kat and Gunnar, realizing Ash was no longer part of the conversation, looked around the room. They saw him over by the sandwiches, filling a plate with more than any one teenager could possibly eat. And, thinking no one was looking, filling his pockets with pre-wrapped packages of granola bars and cookies.

A look passed between Gunnar and Kat. Had this boy been stealing money and valuables to put food on his grandmother's table?

CHAPTER 19

"She was confused and disoriented," the agent from West Gorge Human Services told Kat on the phone the next morning, after paying a visit to Ash's granny. "It was apparent she hadn't been eating or taking her medications. We checked her into the West Gorge Nursing Home to stabilize her, and will determine next steps.

Kat had a knot in her stomach at the thought of telling Ash that his only relative would no longer be able to care for him. Granny could barely take care of herself. For now, she would give Ash a cursory update, but wait until she had more news before alarming him.

Speaking of news, she would have to gussy up a bit and face a press event that the hospital was staging. The poor PR team was at a breaking point—they did not have all the answers people wanted. And like it or not, that was a hat Kat was going to have to wear.

"We have to maintain the public's trust," Shep told her on the phone when she protested. She didn't mind talking to the press, but she had so little time to set aside.

"All right," she relented, "I can do that."

Kat had watched her mentor deftly handle reporters, and felt confident. After all, the little *West Gorge Weekly* was hardly the *Tri-City*

News. There was no scandal to unearth, only people who were sick, recovering, or caught in the crosshairs.

Speaking of which, Kat noticed that Gunnar and Ash seemed to be amiable enough this morning. She had walked in to the break room for coffee to find the two of them cleaning and organizing the food and the boxes. They had even charmed the scrapbook ladies into helping them bring a sense of order to the room.

"Can I toast you a bagel?" One of the ladies asked Kat when she walked in. She wore a name tag that said *Marta* as she stood behind a makeshift counter and poured the doctor her coffee. "Cream and sugar are behind you."

"Just like Starbucks. Thank you, Marta," Kat said, appreciatively. She recognized the woman who ran the hospital gift shop.

"Gunnar told us you were up all night tending to poor Belle Wild," Marta said. "It's the least we can do."

Kat nodded and glanced across the room at the cowboy, who had his back to her. She had been up most of the night with Belle, and a few other patients who reacted strongly to the virus. Josh, she knew, was exhausted, so she sent him to get some sleep.

"Is she any better this morning, Doctor Tate?" Another woman, whose name tag read *June*, asked. "I've known Belle all my life," she continued, with a catch in her voice. "She taught Sunday school when I was little."

Marta nodded alongside June, as she handed Kat the toasted bagel with cream cheese.

Kat knew she shouldn't discuss a patient's condition with anyone who wasn't family. But looking at the concern on the faces of Marta and June, who only got caught in the quarantine because of new inventory for the little gift shop, she bent the rules. They were all in this together, she justified.

"Keep Belle in your prayers, ladies," she said. "Today will be critical for her."

Kat thanked the women again and turned to go check on Belle. She had been sick too long. This virus was a white-hot fever that burnt out quickly—or should, anyway.

. . .

WHILE BELLE WILD WRESTLED WITH HER SHARP FEVER, TWO OTHER patients in her room showed marked improvement in their conditions. They could soon join others in a recovery area of the wing, while a few of those recovering could be moved to rooms where they could begin to care for themselves again.

This would be a relief to the overworked nurses and medical staff.

Kat would ask for volunteers to help the recovered patients who were no longer contagious, only weak and tired. If they could be brought a bowl of soup or a sandwich every now and then, they would begin to feel stronger before the quarantine's end.

It was Kat's hope that most every patient would be considered "recovered" in just a few days, so the quarantine could end and they could all go home. She longed for the grand apartment and her own bed; her favorite reading chair and her granite countertops.

She could gaze at the mountain range while scrambling eggs and sautéing fresh asparagus from the farmer's market in West Gorge. Kat thought she'd go on the hunt for a bicycle that she could ride back and forth to the market—one with a large basket on the front.

In happier times, while growing up, Kat and her parents would often ride their bikes to the farm markets to stock up on seasonal corn right from the harvest, as well as peaches, blueberries and tomatoes.

While in med school, and working at City General, she had to be satisfied with quick ingredients from the mini-marts. The few things she did manage to find fresh on the streets tasted like exhaust from the cars and taxis by the time she got home to her efficiency walk-up.

But this was a new life, away from the big buildings and traffic.

Kat could breathe out here in Wyoming. She hoped to build a life, and maybe have a family of her own someday. In the meantime, there were beautiful spots along the gorge and the foothills where Kat would like to explore and have picnics—and not always by herself.

She was so used to being alone and lonely. But there was something about West Gorge that gave her a new sense of hope, and an openness about finding love.

It could prove to be more challenging than she had expected, though, especially if all the men out here were thick-necked cowboys. Is that what she could expect—rough and ready *good ol' boys* like Gunnar West? All hands and no conversation? Kat sure hoped not.

Her heart sank at the prospect of having to settle for a cowboy. What would that make her—Mrs. Cowboy? *Doctor Cowgirl?* Would they sign their Christmas cards "Doctor and Mister Cowboy?"

Then again, maybe that wouldn't be so bad. Perhaps cowboys proved to be more faithful and loyal to their families than car salesmen. They couldn't be any worse. Kat would never forget the day she learned that her father, after taking a pretty young thing out for a test drive, had chosen to kick the old model to the curb.

CHAPTER 20

"ResVi is a highly contagious virus, Layne," Kat was saying into the computer monitor in the hospital lobby. She was on a two-way live newsfeed with Layne Jenkins from the *West Gorge Weekly*, being broadcast on the local news. "And to answer your question, yes, most people were taken aback at being quarantined here in the north wing."

Layne was nodding, Kat could see, encouraging her to go on. About a dozen people stood quietly off to the side, including Doctor Josh Quell, a few of the nurses, and the scrapbook ladies. Gunnar West and Ash stood nearby, too.

"But people quickly rallied," she said, with a nod to the room, "and everyone is pitching in where they can to make the best of a bad situation."

"Doctor Tate," Layne asked, "how can we prevent the spread of this virus in the community?"

That's right Layne, Kat thought, keep pitching me softballs and let's get through this.

"Good question, Layne," Kat said with a plastered-on smile. "This quarantine is the best step we can take to make sure most of the contagion disperses within these walls. But that doesn't mean others outside of the hospital weren't exposed. So, wash your hands often, limit large gatherings for the next week, and if you have any of the symptoms being displayed on your monitor, call your doctor."

"Thank you, Doctor Tate," Layne said. "Check the station's website for more information. And doctor... one more question."

"Shoot," Kat said, feeling proud of successfully wrapping up her first solo performance.

"We hear that local resident, Belle Wild, is in critical condition with the virus, and may not make it through the day. Belle's family was alarmed to hear this news from a source inside your walls, and they are inconsolable. Would you care to comment?"

Kat froze.

Seconds passed as she stared at the monitor like a deer caught in the headlights. If she didn't rally, and fast, this clip was going to go viral.

Kat forced herself to speak.

"Layne," she said, scrambling for the right words, "I can't discuss any patient's condition, but thank you for your concern. I will personally call the family of every patient who has contracted the virus and give them an update."

After signing off, Kat turned to look at Marta and June, who could only shrug.

"We added her to the prayer chain," Marta said, sheepishly.

"You said it was critical," June added.

"Are you mad at us, Doctor Tate?" Marta asked.

Kat had forgotten how small-town prayer chains could travel at the speed of light—almost as fast as a tuna noodle casserole could travel from an oven to a church picnic.

"I'm not mad," Kat said. "She should absolutely be on the prayer chain." But she knew she had breached a code of ethics and was silently kicking herself.

After nearly everyone wandered off, including Marta and June, Kat was left feeling deflated, sitting in the lobby by herself. Looking up, she saw Gunnar West. He held out a bottle of cold Ginger Ale and indicated a chair nearby.

Great, Kat thought. Just the person she didn't want to see at this time.

"Truce?" he said.

Kat looked up and shrugged. She took the cold bottle of bubbly soda with gratitude.

"Shep Arndt is going to have my hide," she said to Gunnar. "I never should have talked about a patient to anyone but family. It's just…"

Kat dropped her head into her hands.

"Kat," Gunnar said, "drink the Ginger Ale. You've hardly slept and you need a few calories in your system. Good sugary ones."

She looked up and saw kindness in his eyes—where did that come from? She took a few sips and closed her eyes. It tasted so cold and refreshing.

"It's not my first quarantine," Kat said. "But every time, I feel as though I'm on a desert island, isolated from the real world. Parts of that I don't mind. But I sometimes forget important things, like who I can and can't talk to. And that everyone has a cell phone and connection to the outside world."

"It was an honest mistake, Kat," Gunnar said as he sat near her. "I heard you talking to the ladies this morning, and you did not disclose anything you shouldn't have. They *should* be praying for Belle's recovery, and now many good people are."

Kat nodded and took another drink. She was starting to feel better and calmer. Exhaustion was setting in. She'd have to sleep soon.

"Thank you for that," she told him, "and for this," she said, indicating the cold drink.

Gunnar nodded. He was starting to feel protective of Kat, and realized that he wanted to place his arm around her shoulder and push the wild ringlets back from her face. Her messy bun was lopsided on her head and her professor glasses looked slightly tilted.

She was lovely.

Kat looked again at Gunnar, searching once more for the kindness. Seeing it was still there, she let her guard down. "I'm truly sorry I got you into this mess, Gunnar," she said. "It's my fault you're here. And it's my fault that our date was a disaster."

Gunner was shocked by her unexpected honesty, and his heart clenched as he saw her eyes misting up.

"As you can probably tell," she said, blinking hard, "I don't date much. When Jackie set us up, I was excited just to meet someone and make a new friend. But I ruined it by trying too hard."

Gunnar was surprised at her disclosure and touched by her candor. How could a woman be so accomplished, yet so vulnerable? It made him ashamed of the snap judgment he made when he first saw her, and ashamed of how relieved he was when she got called back to the hospital.

"You're wrong, Kat, I ruined it," he said. "I didn't try hard enough."

CHAPTER 21

*K*at didn't think she could fall asleep. Her thoughts swirled around her head like storm clouds as she sat helplessly in the eye of a tornado, watching.

There was poor Belle, who couldn't seem to break her fever, and Kat's indiscretion in talking about her to non-family. The blindside at the press conference was a result of that, and she really should have known better. Even with Gunnar's grace, she hated to make such a public mistake and didn't want her boss to lose his confidence in her.

Another troubling picture was Ash, who would have to be told soon that his granny was in a nursing home, being treated for dehydration and delusion.

Geriatric medicine was not Kat's field of study, but she knew enough to speculate that granny wasn't coming home—so where did that leave her teenaged grandson? Foster care seemed like a hard blow to a kid who had nobody, and who was struggling with staying on the right side of the law.

Finally, there was the confusing conversation with the cowboy— the big galoot who was almost always mad at her, but had been right there to encourage her when she needed it after the press conference.

In spite of being a member of the hospital board, he supported her in her fumble. Maybe that's why she let her defenses down with him.

Kat was very tired. Over tired, as her mother used to say when she was a child. So tired she was finding it difficult to control her emotions, which explained her unsettling desire to have a second chance with Gunnar, the cowboy who couldn't stand her. She tossed and turned with that desire.

What she really wanted was for him to put his strong arms around her and just hold her, like he had the other night when she stumbled into him. She wanted to breathe in the earthy scent of his cowboy shirt, the one that embarrassed her on their date a few nights before, and let his strength and confidence drive away all her fears and insecurities.

Slowly winding down, Kat allowed herself to shut off all the images and fall asleep—just as she had trained herself to do in med school. She had already lost a full thirty minutes of her four-hour sleep window, and she couldn't afford to lose any more.

"Doctor Tate, you'd better wake up." Josh Quell was speaking in a low but urgent tone. Lifting her eye mask, Kat looked at his furled brow and worried eyes.

"Is it Belle?" she asked, and Josh nodded in the affirmative.

"Shoot," she said, sitting bolt upright. "Is she..."

"She's alive, but getting worse," he said.

All the other virus sufferers presented textbook symptoms. They had fever and chills, aches and pains, and trouble breathing at times, which was worrisome. Most had dangerous fever spikes and then... blessed signs of recovery, followed by weakness and exhaustion.

All except Belle.

"I'll call Shep," she told Josh.

The director of West Gorge Medical Center had given his star infectious disease specialist a Hot Line phone number when she signed on. He would always have this phone on him, he said; it would always be charged and by his side.

Only he and his wife, Arlene Arndt, knew that this phone number was mostly a placebo—it gave him the appearance of being accessible, but the phone hardly ever rang. True emergencies were rare in West Gorge, and most others on the staff and hospital board just called his regular phone line.

When Shep's phone rang on his nightstand, he was crawling into bed with a good detective novel. He shot a surprised look at Arlene and knew it must be Kat.

"Talk to me, Doctor Tate," Shep said as he answered.

"Shep, one of our original virus patients is not recovering. Looking at her history, I suspect she has an underlying heart valve condition that can't be treated in the north wing. She may need surgery, and fast," Kat said. "But with the fever, she's highly contagious."

"What you're saying is that to save the patient," Shep said, "we have to expose the surgical wing and additional medical staff to the virus."

"I doubt she'll live through the night otherwise," Kat said, simply.

At that, Shep hung up to call the Chief of Surgery. Within minutes, they put an unprecedented plan in motion—first, they'd reschedule all elective surgeries, and then move recovering patients to another wing. Once that was accomplished, the surgical team would don the hazmat-type full body protective suits and breach the quarantined wing.

Belle Wild would head to surgery, and the surgical wing would then become a secondary quarantine site.

After hanging up the phone, Shep traded his pajamas for khakis and a sweater, and Arlene Arndt went to put on a pot of coffee. It was going to be a long night.

CHAPTER 22

*I*n the dark quiet of the night, Kat made her way into the break room, looking for more than just a snack. It was nearly midnight and the first moment she'd been able to breath or eat since her morning bagel.

Turning the light on, she saw a pizza box on the table. Lifting the lid, three cold and shriveled slices stared back at her.

"Well that's a sorry sight," Gunnar was right behind her, looking at the pizza.

"Haven't you eaten?" she turned to ask him.

"No time," he said, "I've been on the phone with the hospital board and with Shep, and some of the medical staff. Belle Wild's complications have been complicated for everyone. But she's been safely moved, and is in surgery right now."

"Not a moment too soon," Kat said, and smiled a weary smile.

Gunnar nodded sympathetically.

"You've taken great care of her, Kat," he said. "She's in good hands with our surgeons."

It was Kat's turn to nod. She hoped Gunnar was right.

"And don't forget," he said, "Belle is on the West Gorge prayer chain."

She smiled at him with genuine relief. She did not want to have any casualties with this virus and had grown fond of her patient. At least now, Belle had a better chance of survival. With her number one worry in capable hands, Kat was free to rest for a moment in Gunnar's assurances—until her grumbling stomach broke the spell.

"I'm starving!" Kat said with a laugh.

"Me too," he said. "Tell me what you're hungry for and I'll get a delivery."

"It's so late, I don't think anything will be open," Kat said.

"West Gorge is the city that never sleeps," Gunnar said. "Didn't Shep tell you that?"

"I thought that was New York," Kat replied with a small laugh.

"Maybe you're right," Gunnar smiled, "but I know a few people in West Gorge who stay up pretty late, so tell me what you want."

"Well... what I've really been craving," she said, "is BBQ ribs."

Forty minutes later, Kat and Gunnar sat on the floor of an empty office at the very far corner of the wing. She had taken him to her secret hideaway, where no one thought to look for anyone. The only furniture was a desk and a loveseat, so they threw the two sofa cushions on the floor, and sat down facing each other, with legs stretched out in front of them.

"You must know somebody," Kat said as she eyed the big bag from Red's Rib Shack.

"I have friends in the right places, Kat," Gunnar laughed, "both high and low. Red Carter is one of my high school football buddies, and you and I both know his wife, Jackie. Red always had a grill going back then and still does."

"It smells amazing," Kat said, as she helped unpack the feast. "Fair warning, I'm going to fight you for each and every rib."

Gunnar shot a look at Kat that she didn't know how to interpret— it looked like respect, but that couldn't be right.

After a few bites of ribs, beans, cornbread and slaw, Gunnar broke the silence.

"I'm just glad you didn't want any fussy little pasta puffs."

Kat raised her eyebrows and glanced up from the rib in her hands. She had sauce on her arm and hands and probably her face, but she didn't care.

"Are you poking holes in our date, Gunnar West?" Kat asked him in a teasing voice.

He smiled at her.

"I told you," she went on, "I'm new in town and didn't have much to go on."

"Well, then why didn't you let me choose?" he asked. "This is my town."

"I should have," she answered. "As I said, dating is new for me and I'm not good at it."

"Practice makes perfect," Gunnar said with a grin.

Kat considered that, and enjoyed seeing the cowboy's smile.

"Have you dated much?" Kat asked him, taking another piece of cornbread.

"I guess so." Gunnar answered cautiously. "I don't want you to think I date too much, or too freely. Maybe there was a time when I did, but I've actually become more conservative, I suppose."

"Well," Kat ventured in between bites of slaw, "then practice doesn't amount to much, Gunnar, because you weren't any better at our date than I was."

Gunnar frowned and opened his mouth to protest. But with one look at the mischievous twinkle in Kat's eye, he must have known she was pulling his leg.

He exhaled and relaxed again.

"I reckon you're right, Kat," he said.

Kat was glad he could take a little ribbing; that he wasn't always a powder keg about to go off. After learning about his mother passing away, most likely in this hospital, Kat had put two and two together. Of course he wouldn't want to be trapped here with those memories. That was likely a factor in the way he reacted to the quarantine.

She moved the conversation on and asked him about his ranch. Gunnar told her about the cattle and the horses, the livestock and the gardens, and the people on West Ranch. She wanted to hear more about Ridge and his two younger brothers.

She was interested in his ancestors and how they settled the land and built the town.

Kat was impressed with his business degree, and regretted thinking that he was beneath her, somehow, simply because of the way he was dressed. She had been very wrong. And when he talked with great pride about mentoring teens at the high school, she thought about Ash—she'd have to remember to update Gunnar about the boy's situation.

Kat answered his questions about her family in Illinois.

She casually mentioned that her parents divorced, but left out the part about her mother begging her dad to stay all those years ago; how she had clawed and grabbed at his packed suitcase like a wild animal as he made his way to his car, while Kat watched in horror from her bedroom window.

Gunnar asked Kat about med school and her position at City General. He asked her why she went into the field of infectious diseases.

"Relationships," she answered. "Viruses and contagions are about the relationship between germs and people, and between people and other people. While I can't always figure life out, Gunnar, things that are under a microscope seem to make sense to me."

Gunnar looked at the beautiful doctor, with her hair piled on her head and BBQ sauce on one of her cheeks, and smiled. He began to lift his hand gently toward her face, then caught himself.

"Don't underestimate your power with people, Kat," he said. "You have a way with your patients and staff, and even with the other innocent bystanders at the hospital. You're a natural leader and people feel confident following you."

Kat was mesmerized by both Gunnar's words and the deep sound of his voice—she couldn't take her eyes off his mouth as he spoke, and the way his kind eyes crinkled slightly when he talked.

She wanted to reach over and touch his tanned face and the thick curls in his hair.

Why had she thought he was a Neanderthal—a *big lug*? He was smart and thoughtful. He built people up and didn't blow his own horn, although clearly, he had every right to.

After they had thoroughly wiped the BBQ sauce off their hands and faces with wet wipes sent by Red, Gunnar stood up and reached down for Kat's hands to help her to her feet. Somehow when she stood, they ended up very close to each other, and more than anything Kat wanted to feel his arms around her again, but she couldn't dare ask.

Kat knew that if he embraced her again, she'd never want to leave his arms.

Standing and facing each other, still hand in hand, Gunnar held her eyes in his for what seemed like a long time. Long enough for her to feel both comfortable and unsettled. Then he slowly raised her hands up to his lips and gently kissed them.

"Sheriff," he said, softly, "when you finally let me out of this jail, would you do me the honor of going out with me?"

A chill ran up Kat's spine as she found herself leaning into Gunnar and lifting her face up to his. She was sure he was about to kiss her, and in spite of the warning bells going off in her head, she welcomed it.

Kat was lonely and wanted to be kissed. And that's all it would be, just a kiss. Just a break in the long dry streak that was her love life.

This wasn't her first quarantine; she had witnessed plenty of people creating romantic scenarios out of thin air to break the monotony of being closed in, though she'd never taken part in the antics before.

Gunnar West was simply trading his anger for boredom, and saw her as a diversion. If she could keep her heart out of the transaction, maybe it would be fun to share an innocent kiss or two, in between writing prescriptions and updating medical charts.

His invitation for a date was sincere in the heat of the moment, and surely something they'd both agree was not necessary once she did let Gunnar out of her "jail." For now, it would make their kiss seem honorable.

But as her lips just barely brushed his beautiful mouth, her phone rang harshly, which caused them to freeze. She was being beckoned to her nightly patient rounds.

"Thank you for dinner, Gunnar." Kat whispered as she dropped his hands and bolted out the door.

CHAPTER 23

*B*ig city living had not been as glamorous as Darlene Shire imagined it would be. Housing and other costs were outrageously expensive—she barely had enough money to pay her utility bills and buy groceries every week.

She had zero dollars in her budget for new clothes, but how could she *not* buy new things after the way her boss and co-workers looked down at her western-style shirts and jeans.

"A little of that look goes a long way, Darlene," her editor had said on her second week.

As a result, she had to take her emergency credit cards on a shopping spree, and now she was drowning in the minimum payments and interest charges.

Darlene wanted to do more than just live and work.

She wanted to go out on the town with her new friends and colleagues, but that was out of her reach. For what she spent on one mixed drink in the city, she could have an entire rib dinner at Red's back home—not that she ever picked up the bill. Gunnar wouldn't let her. But that was beside the point.

The staff from the *Tri-City News* went to a bar named Blue Moon every Friday. They'd have multiple drinks with "small plates" of appetizers while Darlene would nurse a seltzer water and pretend she wasn't hungry. She had learned the hard way that the small plates came with a big price tag.

"Won't you eat, Darlene?" They all coaxed and goaded her as her stomach growled.

"We hate to eat in front of you," they'd say.

She knew it was a trap, though. The first time she joined them, she ate two fried wontons and three tortilla chips with salsa—then someone suggested they all split the bill, for convenience. Darlene had been forced to chip in the $30 she had in her pocket for her weekend grocery run, and only got a few nibbles in return.

It was a costly lesson.

Where did these kids get all their money? Darlene wasn't old—slightly past her mid-thirties—but she suspected the twenty somethings from the paper all lived at home still. Their income was disposable, while hers was budgeted to the penny.

But if she didn't go to the Blue Moon, she felt disconnected from this young group of ambitious millennials. On Monday mornings they'd be laughing at inside jokes and antics from their night on the town, while Darlene would be on the outside looking in.

Sometimes, they'd talk about work at the bar on Friday nights. They'd divvy up assignments and toss around ideas for upcoming special issues and newspaper spreads, leaving anyone out who wasn't there. That was usually Darlene.

"Exciting and invigorating," is how Darlene described her life to friends back home.

Competitive and exhausting, that was the truth of it all.

And so, as Darlene faced the choice of whether to renew her apartment lease for another six months or not, she began thinking about going home to West Gorge.

"Not with my tail between my legs, though," she promised herself. Her editor had first put the bug in her ear, by mentioning a story that was starting to get some attention.

"Hey, Darlene," she said, "aren't you from West Gorge? Are you tracking that story about the hospital shutting an entire wing down for this virus? Now they're closing the surgical wing. Some new doctor is in charge, and a few dozen locals are quarantined."

Darlene's sister, Daisy, posted a few comments on her social site, but Darlene hadn't thought much of it. Now, her editor said she should go back home to cover the story.

"Seems the virus originated in your town," she said. "Maybe there's a story there."

By *story*, her editor meant *scandal*, she was sure.

Scandals were everything in the current newspaper world, Darlene was finding out. With the demand for printed papers on the decline, the real money was made through their digital sites. Many reporters now got paid by the number of "clicks" on an article, so the temptation was there to make everything a scandal.

Sadly, this encouraged reporters to inject the whisper of gossip and intrigue into everyday events—like school board meetings. If they could photograph someone mid-sneeze, they could post a picture that looked like anger or discord, with a headline to match, such as:

Did the Board Go Too Far This Time?

JOURNALISM HAD BECOME A RIDICULOUS WORLD SINCE SHE GOT HER degree, and Darlene didn't always recognize it. Plus, she found it hard to bake scandal into her articles, at least the ones she was used to writing. The ones that the paper had hired her to write.

Get the Farmhouse Look for Less had been popular, but there was no gossip there.

Brunch on the Ranch got some clicks, and her editor liked the story. But on the Monday morning after being published, Darlene overheard the younger reporters snickering, and making an unkind comment about her "cowboy content."

"Readers are over it," one of them said to another.

And perhaps the world was over it; maybe they'd moved on to articles about green living and tiny little houses. Darlene knew she would never be "on trend" if trends included eco-vacations and vegan weddings.

She felt so removed from her colleagues and what they cared about. She was tired of pretending and scrambling to keep up. She was tired of being broke, and away from her home and family.

Maybe it was time to head back to West Gorge, Darlene thought.

Maybe it was time to marry Gunnar West.

CHAPTER 24

Gunnar had been a real catch for Darlene Shire, whose father was a pharmacist that owned the corner drugstore in West Gorge.

"Tread carefully, Dar," her father warned when they started dating. "Gunnar West is an important man in this town. Don't drag him or our family through any of your drama."

Darlene only laughed at her dad's caution, but his words came back when she inevitably hurt Gunnar's feelings. She could still picture the look on his face when she told him she was leaving to work in the city, to build up her name as a reporter and writer.

He was surprised, for sure.

What bothered her the most was that Gunnar almost looked relieved, and that's what she couldn't shake. That didn't make sense at all to Darlene, because she was sure he was about to propose marriage.

Gunnar had begun asking Darlene frightening questions—what she thought about commitment and careers. Did she have a favorite charity and did she like to volunteer with the needy—what did she think about *children*, for crying out loud.

It was only natural, she supposed. They had been together for two full years. While they bickered like an old married couple, he must have figured they should make it official.

But *babies*?

Lord no.

Darlene had some oats to sow before she was going to show up at church in her Sunday best as a West bride, and mind her manners 'til death or divorce parted them. And she sure had things to do before there was ever talk of a baby.

The new job had seemed like a perfect opportunity to put some space in between the Shires and the Wests, as it were. To let their liaison breath.

"If he and I are meant to be," she told her pretty twin sister, Daisy, "it's meant to be."

Unlikely as it was, a growing news story about a quarantine in her home town seemed to point to her and Gunnar being "meant to be." Especially after finding out her rent was increasing for the city apartment, coupled with Daisy telling her that one of the quarantined locals was none other than Gunnar himself.

"Well, I'll be," she hooted to Daisy, knowing how much Gunnar hated to be confined. "He must be chomping at the bit, penned up in the hospital like a wild mustang."

She did feel sorry for just a moment, thinking about how Gunnar's mother had died in that hospital only a year before the two of them started dating. Darlene knew that it was Gunnar's least favorite place —one he avoided when he could.

This naturally led her to think about Randi West herself, the larger-than-life, legendary benefactor, philanthropist, and beloved patron saint to the community of West Gorge.

"Those are big lady boots to fill," she said out loud as she packed her car to come home. Whoever married Gunnar West was going to be held to an impossibly high standard, she knew. But anybody could be good when they were as wealthy as the West family, she thought.

Anyone could do all those good things when they had a nearly unlimited supply of money to work with, Darlene figured. And there would still be plenty of money left over to do the things a girl wanted to do, like travel, and buy some nice clothes and jewelry.

"Mrs. West," Darlene said out loud, trying the title on like a new sweater. Maybe she shouldn't have been so quick to walk away from what was nearly a sure thing, a marriage to the most eligible man in West Gorge. Maybe Wyoming.

She could bring a woman's touch to the over-the-top West Ranch house—she'd fly an exclusive decorator in from the city and re-do the place from top to bottom. She'd have lifestyle magazines falling over themselves for the rights to the photo spread.

At that thought, Darlene smiled to think of her own editor and co-workers wooing her for an exclusive article. She couldn't wait to say to them, "Why, my little old ranch renovation is nothing more than *cowboy content*. And you said yourself, your readers are so over it."

Maybe she'd buy the town newspaper outright and be the editor herself—that would be fun. She didn't have to go broke in the city, rolling a big rock uphill just to get a little byline on an article about cast iron fry pans. With West money at her disposal, Darlene could build her own publishing empire, right in her backyard.

Yes, being the mistress of the West fortune was starting to grow on Darlene.

Ridge and the brothers could remain at the ranch house after she and Gunnar married, for a while, anyway. There were lots of wings and suites under that big cedar shake roof. As long as they didn't park their muddy boots and hats on her new furniture.

The old ranch cook would have to go, though. Mrs. West, as Darlene was beginning to think of herself, wouldn't want a dusty old ranch hand cooking steaks and hash in her new designer kitchen.

"You understand I'm sure, Jacob... or Jackson... whatever your name is," Darlene would say to the cook when she fired him. "The Wests need a chef, not a cook; someone to prepare lighter meals and luncheon salads." She would surely entertain some of the women in town and wives from the other big ranches—though no other ranch was as big as hers.

Darlene would hire someone who knew how to delicately core a tomato for a salmon salad cup, and carve radishes into tiny rosettes.

Driving home in her packed little Honda, the next chapter of her life started to write itself, as did the story she would write for the paper. A very click-worthy story.

It wasn't about saving the planet, or recycling, or reducing her carbon footprint. It wasn't about living in a tiny house—just the opposite. The story was about living in a very large house, the largest in the county, the West Ranch.

The headline wrote itself:

Reporter Cheers Up Quarantined Cowboy by Accepting Marriage Proposal

CHAPTER 25

"Good news," Kat said to the assembly gathered in the hospital lobby. "Belle Wild had her emergency surgery, and she is expected to have a full recovery."

The group all gave a little cheer and Kat tried not to catch Gunnar's eye as he stood towards the back. It was the morning after their rib dinner, and all she wanted to think about was their near kiss. But she needed to keep her head in the game.

"Thank God for the prayer chain," Marta said. She was without her friend June, who had presented a fever in the wee hours of the night, according to Doctor Quell.

"I agree, Marta," Kat said, "but I also have bad news. June has come down with a fever, meaning a few more of you have been exposed." The group in the lobby groaned. "But that's why we're all in here, so get your rest, wash your hands, and lay low," Kat said. "If you start to feel sick, let someone know right away."

"Can I go and sit with June, Doctor Tate?" Marta wanted to know.

"That's up to you, Marta," Kat said. "You've been close to June, so it's too late to avoid exposure. You may be immune, but there's no way I can tell just yet."

Marta nodded, and thought of grabbing something for June from the gift shop.

"But take heart, everyone," Kat said. "Other than Belle, our patients have progressed as expected, with a spiked fever and some respiratory issues, followed by full recoveries."

And it was true that they had more people in recovery now than actual patients, so the arc of the virus was beginning to go down and would soon flatten altogether.

This was the good news she would share with Shep in their phone call later that day. Kat got the feeling he was taking some heat from the hospital board over their decision to quarantine—especially with the scrambling the hospital had to do to move Belle into the surgical wing.

Now, they had a secondary quarantined area, and a surgical team that was out of commission until after they either contracted the virus, or tested for immunity.

People started to complain of being inconvenienced. They had to reschedule their appointments and their biopsies, and their mole removals. Their non-life-threatening procedures. They didn't think about ending up like Belle, with a virus that caused major complications to their health and recovery.

It really was a miracle that Belle survived. The odds had not been in her favor.

Kat took a deep breath to clear the stress that was building in the pit of her stomach. Medicine and politics were strange bedfellows, she thought, but the two always went hand in hand. Especially when it came to infectious diseases, and tactics to keep communities safe. There was always someone who wanted to rile people up and cause them to second guess decisions.

As everyone cleared out of the lobby, Kat looked up to find Gunnar lingering.

"Where's Ash?" she asked him.

"He's in the break room," Gunnar said. "I taught him to play poker, and he's got a game going with Marta and a few others."

"Good grief," Kat said, "I hope he's not taking their watches and their phones."

"At least he'd be winning them," Gunnar said with a smile, "and not stealing them."

Kat tried to smile, but felt weary.

"I need to talk to you about Ash," she said. "Can you meet me in ten minutes?"

Gunnar knew where Kat wanted to meet, and in spite of himself, his pulse raced thinking about what had passed between he and Kat last night. And what might be ahead.

He stopped in the break room and poured two hot coffees and grabbed an apple from the fruit bowl. Ash was laying down his cards and saying "full house!" to the table of poker players as they groaned. Someone asked him if he had an ace up his sleeve, but it was good-natured ribbing and Ash looked happy for once.

The kid needed a win in his life, Gunnar suspected, even if the ante was a pile of mini cheese crackers shaped like fish.

CHAPTER 26

Gunnar walked into Kat's hiding place—the unused office at the far end of a quiet hallway—and closed the door behind him. Kat was sitting on top of the desk, rubbing her tired face with her hands. She had her legs pulled up against her body and even in scrubs, her lovely curves were evident.

He wondered how a woman could be sexier in hospital scrubs than a cocktail dress.

"Coffee and an apple," he said, and set them next to her. He was close enough to smell the sweet soap from her morning shower. Her hair was still damp and smelled like honey and apricots. He wanted to linger, but had no right.

Maybe if he had been more of a gentleman on their first date, she would have allowed him to kiss her last night. And then he could nuzzle his face in her neck and skin and hair this very moment, which was his sudden desire.

But he had been clumsy with her sweet and lonely heart.

Gunnar picked up his cup and walked over to the loveseat. He had replaced the cushions before he left last night, just after he almost kissed her. When she had silently leaned in closer and closer into him...

Kat looked up with gratitude and lifted the cup.

"Cheers, cowboy," she said before taking a sip.

"Cheers, sheriff," Gunnar said in return.

She ventured a glance at Gunnar while sipping her coffee. He was wearing a clean buttoned shirt and jeans, and was without his boots and hat. He smelled fresh, like a breeze off the mountains. And his rugged tanned face had been shaved and scrubbed.

It had been all she could do to keep herself from grabbing his strong arms when he was near just now, and wrapping them around her waist. She wanted to pull herself right into him again and find his lips with her own.

Last night was sweet, but it wasn't her hands that needed kissing!

She had been too quick to judge him on their first date. Would that forever haunt them? All signs indicated he was willing to overlook her inept behavior and give them another chance. But when he heard what she had to say, it might change everything.

AFTER DRINKING COFFEE AND GATHERING HER THOUGHTS, KAT WAS ready to talk.

"I filled you in on Ash's home life," she told Gunnar, "but it's gotten complicated."

Kat then told him about requesting a wellness visit for Ash's granny after the off-handed comments the boy had made. As a result, she was indeed diagnosed with dementia and could no longer look after herself, or her grandson.

She would be in the nursing home indefinitely, Kat told Gunnar.

"Ash needs to be told that he doesn't have a home to go home to when the doors open again," Kat said. "Because he's still 15, he will have to go into foster care."

She could tell by Gunnar's face that they shared the same concern —Ash would be miserable in foster care. He would more than likely run away and have an even tougher life than the one he already led.

"I'll tell him," Gunnar said. "That's hard news for the boy, and I'm sorry for him. I really am. But he should hear it from me."

Kat nodded. After Gunnar's initial rebellion, he took his job seriously, staying close to Ash at all times. The two of them joked around as they helped where they could, keeping the spirits up of those around them.

Gunnar made Ash his co-conspirator when it came to choosing and ordering carry-out dinners from the town's restaurants. And Gunnar was determined to show the boy the "art of manhood," by teaching him poker, good manners and chivalry.

"No woman should walk through a door behind you, kid," she'd heard Gunnar tell him.

Kat wondered if Gunnar was going to teach Ash how to help a lady into a pickup truck. But before she could allow her thoughts to wander to their ill-fated blind date, she had to finish this serious conversation.

She told Gunnar that a social worker would meet Ash at the hospital when the quarantine was lifted—in three or four days, most likely.

"They'll try to find him a home in proximity to school," Kat continued. "His attendance has been spotty, understandably, but the principal said he's a very bright and gifted kid."

Gunnar raised his eyebrows and nodded at this.

Taking a few sips of her coffee again, Kat knew it was time to change the subject.

"Gunnar," Kat ventured carefully, "when people are in a confined space for any length of time, the mind can play tricks. I've witnessed the way rules and morals can fly out the window, even though everybody knows it's temporary."

"You said it was like being on a desert island," Gunnar said.

"Exactly," Kat said. "But the truth is, this quarantine will be over in a few days and we all go back to the real world."

"And?" Gunnar asked, not knowing for sure what point Kat was making.

"And, we were pretty close to kissing last night," Kat said. "At least, I wanted to kiss you."

Gunnar held his breath silently. He still wanted that kiss.

"I just don't want the two of us to write a check on a desert island," Kat said, "that we can't cash once we're rescued."

CHAPTER 27

"It's a snow storm out here, Kat," Shep was saying on the phone, "and I don't mean *snow*. I've got patients calling and yelling that they can't have their elective surgeries, and families crying at me because they can't see their loved ones in the hospital. I've got a surgical team that's out of commission. Board members are squawking at me and the press is hounding me."

"I'm sorry about your troubles, Shep," Kat said. "This virus is a relentless enemy."

"I know," he said. "But some are saying we overreacted and shut down too fast."

Kat knew this argument well. With every community-wide epidemic or pandemic, the Monday morning quarterbacks and the second-guessers had nothing better to do than plant seeds of doubt in everyone's mind. It was her job to stand by her own convictions and give Shep reasons to do the same.

"Shep," Kat said, "we did our job *too* well. That's why you're getting a world of grief."

Shep didn't respond, but she knew he was listening. He wanted more than anything to hear solid reasons to keep standing behind her in this quarantine.

"If we had waited any longer to make the hard decisions," Kat told him, "many more people in our community would be affected. Then they'd be yelling at you for other reasons—asking why we weren't more proactive. Especially after hiring me."

"Mmm," Shep murmured neutrally.

"We acted quickly," she said. "And because we did, we sent the virus packing, on a tour bus. Leaving the residents of West Gorge inconvenienced but not devastated."

"Thanks for the talking points, Kat," Shep said, "it will help with the press."

Kat could hear the relief and reassurance in his voice, and knew she'd been successful. But this was not her first rodeo. Things were calm now, but something could go very wrong. Especially with the press. Any emergency situation was a bit like a staring contest. The press pretended to be supportive while constantly digging for dirt.

"Speaking of the press," Shep said, "a reporter from the *Tri-City News* wants to talk."

"To me?" Kat wondered why such a large paper would want to talk to her.

"She has local roots, apparently," Shep said, "but writes mainly for the feature section. She's probably doing a puff piece on what you're eating, that kind of thing."

"Huh," Kat said. Now it was her turn to be cajoled a bit.

"By the way," Shep said, "what are you eating—are you getting everything you need?"

Kat thought of the rib dinner Gunnar ordered in the middle of the night, and set up like a picnic in her favorite hideaway spot. Sitting on the floor, facing each other, the world faded away for Kat. She and Gunnar could just as easily have been leaning against a tree, sitting on a bed of clover along the edge of the West Gorge River.

She thought of the sauce dripping down her arm, and how she'd snatched up the last rib without any thought of being ladylike. Kat could still picture the gleam in Gunnar's eyes as he watched her appreciatively devour the feast.

She had been famished, hungry and greedy—and Gunnar loved it.

"Kat? Did I lose you?" It was Shep interrupting her thoughts.

"I'm doing fine, Shep," she said at last. "I'm eating like a cowgirl."

CHAPTER 28

heers, cowboy.

The simple statement, spoken by the beautiful Kat Tate, was playing through Gunnar West's mind like a ribbon of fog along the mighty gorge. But unlike a fog, Gunnar felt more clear-headed than he'd been in years. He began seeing his life with a new perspective.

He wanted to be somebody a woman like Kat could count on. Could he be that man?

Gunnar sat in the hidden office with his eyes closed, thinking about Kat and what she said. He thought about his desire to wrap his arms around her and hold her tight. He thought about inviting her to the ranch and introducing him to his father and brothers—showing her every mile of the West property, from the foothills to the river. The grazing acreage. The West hunting camp and the West fishing camp.

There was the guest house and the bunk house.

The cook house doubled as residence for Justice Kemp, and bunk house for any auxiliary staff he had to hire for the annual West BBQ, which saw hundreds of ranchers and townsfolk come in for the day.

The West men would all love Kat, he knew. The woman could hold her own.

Gunnar knew his mama would love Kat. Randi West would have been the first to befriend this newcomer to West Gorge, and invite her to the ranch for a weekend. These women, the doctor and the lawyer, would have been fast friends.

But Gunnar's images of Kat went far beyond friendship.

He could see her standing in the massive ranch kitchen, joking and talking with Justice and discussing the week's menu. In his daydream, Kat was leaning against the 12-foot granite-topped island, wearing one of Gunnar's shirts and sipping coffee, her long tanned legs and bare feet at home on the cool tiled floor.

Gunnar could picture waking up before the sun and seeing Kat walk from the steamy shower into his dressing area—their dressing area—to get ready for work. She'd stop and kiss him along the way and he'd breathe in the scent of honey and apricots.

He wanted to earn the right to breath that scent and savor those kisses.

A smile played on his lips as he pictured Kat more fully and deeply imbedded in his world, and it all seemed very natural and right. But in order for these images to go beyond a daydream, Gunnar knew she couldn't just be a girlfriend.

She would have to become his…

His eyes flew open as he realized what he had been thinking. For while the ranch was a big and sprawling home for the West men, the presence of women had never been casual.

In the two years he dated Darlene Shire, he'd only brought her to the ranch once or twice, and that was to change trucks or shirts. Gunnar could never picture Darlene at home inside the ranch—she was just too prickly. She came in one time to meet Ridge, at Darlene's insistence, and came out criticizing everything, from the chandeliers crafted from fallen elk antlers to the oversized leather chairs next to the stone fireplace in the vaulted great room.

"It suits us just fine, Darlene," Gunnar had said, through gritted teeth. He remembered how proud Randi had been of their home. She wanted rooms that her boys would feel at home in, and had painstakingly ordered customized pieces.

"Oversized chairs for oversized men," Randi once said.

For herself, she designed a more feminine inner office at the ranch with a stunning view of the river, through a window framed in celery silk damask. Randi's had tall wing chairs covered in floral tapestries, and plush white carpet never walked on by anything but clean wool slippers.

The door to this room had remained closed for years, and Gunnar did not open it for Darlene. He didn't trust her with its existence. And yet, it wasn't a stretch to imagine Kat sitting behind his mother's delicate Norwegian pine desk.

He somehow felt that, where Darlene would only see the room for its décor and what she wanted to change, Kat would know how to rightly handle the sacred nature of the space, and understand the place the room held in the hearts of the West men.

Gunnar remembered thinking he had dodged a bullet when he came home from his date with Kat Tate, but could now see that the real bullet had been Darlene.

The two of them fought about everything and nothing at all.

Once, at Red's Rib Shack, he and Darlene had gotten into it and Darlene stormed out. Red came over to Gunnar's table and clapped him hard on the back. "God gives man free rein 'til *woman* reins him in," he said with a booming laugh. "You going' after her?"

Gunnar was irritated. He didn't like it when Darlene aired their dirty laundry in public places. Everyone knew the West family, they owned half the county and should be able to settle their grievances on their own land, and not give townsfolk something to talk about.

And he was not about to take dating advice from Red, even though Red and Jackie were one of the happiest couples Gunnar knew, aside from his own parents.

What really irritated Gunnar was any talk of being reined in. He had never liked the thought of being trapped. That's why, for a time, Darlene had been the perfect girlfriend. She was around when there was a dance or a BBQ. They had fun camping together and riding horses. But when it came to picturing Darlene inside the West Ranch, being part of the West family, that's where the fun stopped.

He was surprised, then relieved, that she followed her dream to the city before their dating had gotten serious—as he was considering it might.

"You stick to ribs, Red," Gunnar had told him, "and I'll stick to women."

But Gunnar didn't stick to women and he was beginning to realize that. For years, he never wanted constraints on the life he greatly enjoyed. He could take a horse or a Jeep anytime he desired and head into the mountains. Or up to one of the many camps and cabins on West land. He valued his freedom.

Later, after Randi passed away, he couldn't imagine opening himself up to that kind of pain—the level of pain that Ridge walked with every moment of his life. Why would any man sign on for the great gulping sobs at losing your other half, and the cold and lonely nights spent missing your sweetheart, the woman you held in your arms each and every night?

He thought that just maybe he was getting closer to that answer. Perhaps when the right woman came into your life, the risks took a backseat to the rewards of love.

Before leaving the little room, Gunnar allowed himself to think about Kat once again and couldn't help but smile. Why was she so endearing? A woman so awkward on a blind date, yet so confident and in charge at the hospital.

She deserved more than a desert island romance. And Gunnar was no longer a boy on Spring break. He was a grown man, closer to 40 than 35. It might just be time to live a grown man's life.

He recalled sitting by his mother's side in the hospital during her final days. She hadn't spoken in a while and Gunnar had his eyes closed for a spell. When he opened them, Randi was looking at him with concern.

"Don't be afraid of life, son," she said as she reached for his hand.

Gunnar remembered thinking she must have meant "don't be

afraid of death," and that her error was a result of the morphine. Then she continued.

"There's always death, Gunnar," Randi said. "But first, there's a sweet, amazing life."

Without a doubt, Randi West had lived a sweet life.

CHAPTER 29

To the tall blonde law school grad of Finnish descent, marriage was something to be deferred indefinitely. Randi Lynn Petersen was just too young and busy to settle down.

Her parents, Waller and Lyllis Petersen, raised Randi in Michigan's Upper Peninsula, along the sweeping shores of Lake Superior.

Gitchegumee, the locals called the lake.

Waller was a third-generation Finnish immigrant, whose ancestors worked in the copper mines. Waller followed in their footsteps for one high school summer, when his foot was crushed by falling ore.

In his grandfather's time, the mine would have provided medical care and then charged him for the rest of his life. He'd "owe his soul to the company store," as the song goes. But the unions had infiltrated copper country, as they had the automotive industry, and Waller's bad fortune turned around.

After graduating from high school with honors and healing from his injury, the mine gave him a scholarship to Northern Michigan University. From there, Waller travelled to the Lower Peninsula and earned his law degree at Michigan State University.

He went back "up north" to work for the mine again. Only this time, it was in a corner office with a window overlooking the lake, not in the deep dark underground.

Randi promised she'd also come back to the Upper Peninsula after law school, as her father had. But her life in Detroit in the 1980s was glamorous and hard to walk away from. Working as an in-house attorney for the Ford Motor Company, she could afford to rent a loft apartment across from the Eastern Market. She enjoyed crossing the Ambassador Bridge into Windsor, Ontario, on weekends. And joining colleagues at the Rooster Tail Restaurant on the Detroit River most Saturday nights. It was a far cry from Stubbs Bar, the local pub back home.

"I'll come home eventually," Randi told her parents, "you'll see."

Waller wanted to believe his daughter. He was anxious for her to meet the new attorney for the mine, the very tall and single Luke Maki. The Petersen's could just picture the beautiful wedding they'd throw for Randi and Luke on the pine-rimmed cliffs of Superior. And they could almost taste the kisses they'd plant on the fresh cheeks of the blonde babies Randi would have.

"Yah, little *lawyer* babies," Lyllis would joke with Waller, and they'd smile.

"At the very least, I'll come for Christmas; for Saint Lucia Day," she told them. "I should be back from my trip by then."

Randi was being sent to Wyoming in an official capacity, to expedite the purchase of a large tract of land by the Ford Motor Company. A Ford executive spotted the West property that was for sale while on a fly-fishing expedition, and thought it a great spot to build a corporate retreat lodge.

Her parents were happy to hear their daughter was coming home for the holidays. They would invite Luke for their Saint Lucia Day feast—the young man and Randi would surely to hit it off. They were both so young and smart; so tall and good looking.

But Luke Maki never came for dinner because Randi never came home.

Ridge West saw to that.

"Who is that goddess?" Ridge said to no one, the first time he set eyes on the willowy attorney from Detroit. Not only was she tall—she was confident enough in her height to wear heels, practically towering over Ridge and his own star struck attorney at their first meeting.

Randi's white-gold hair fell like a waterfall off her shoulders and down her slender back. Her eyes were ice blue, but her smile was warm and comely. As she walked through the law offices of West Properties on her way to the conference room, Ridge saw a string of faces stunned into silence and submission, following her every move.

She owned the room, the meeting, and Ridge himself, without ever saying a word.

The next day, Ridge picked the lawyer up at her hotel in his Land Rover, and drove her to the outfitters in West Gorge for jeans and boots, and a wide-brimmed hat.

"You need to see for yourself what you and Ford Motor Company are buying," he told her. And he convinced her that the best way to survey the land was on horseback.

After a few breathless hours of riding horses over streams and through meadows, along the mountain's edge, Ridge said they should stop for a while and allow the horses to do the same. And that's where the story became West family lore—as Randi would tell her sons about that day, time and time again.

"We came around a large rock, as big as our house, and there in the woods was a table set up next to the gorge," she'd say. "It was set with white linens and speckled tin plates—a luncheon of BBQ chicken and cold salads was waiting for us."

"Underneath a pine sat a cooler of iced Cokes, and Perrier waters with lime wedges," Randi told them, her two favorite drinks in the world ever since.

"As the horses drank from a stream," Randi would say, "Ridge told me about the land and its rich history. About his father and his father's father before him, who claimed West Gorge and made it safe for settlers and families."

Sometimes she would tell the boys the more intimate details—how handsome Ridge looked with his tanned, rugged complexion and thick curly hair that was kissed by the sun. He was a cowboy for sure; a type of man Randi had never crossed paths with. She grew up with tall lanky Finns in Michigan's Upper Peninsula—men who became engineers, miners and loggers; who spent their weekends building cabins and saunas in the woods for their families.

In Detroit, she dated a more gentrified set—lawyers and doctors, and even more engineers, on account of the booming automotive industry in the city. Men who wanted her to pick out a Colonial-style house in West Bloomfield, any one she wanted, and settle into a life in the suburbs with them. A life that held the promise of children and mini vans, tennis and swim clubs, and a yearly ski trip north to Boyne Highlands.

But Randi could never envision her future until she saw Wyoming, and Ridge West.

"I wouldn't kiss him that day," she said, "though I wanted to, badly."

She was determined to keep her professional integrity. Randi Peterson wanted to broker the real estate transaction between Ford and West Properties before her heart became a conflict of interest.

"But as soon as the ink was dry..." she'd say with a laugh.

This would be where Ridge would interject and add to her story, saying that he was sure Randi was more in love with Wyoming, and West Gorge, than with him, but that he would learn to live with being "second fiddle," just to have this beautiful woman in his life.

While he spoke, Randi would gaze at Ridge with a smile that left no doubt that Ridge West was the main attraction for his lover and his bride.

"*Ridge?* What kind of a name is Ridge?" Waller, her father, demanded to know as his plans for his daughter unraveled over the phone. He was unable to hide the panic in his voice.

It was a few weeks after the ride on horseback, and Randi and her parents had been having a tense, long-distance conversation.

"Ridge West," Randi said, simply, "is the name of my husband."

CHAPTER 30

arlene showed up unexpectedly at the front door of the Shire's Craftsman bungalow, and told her mom and dad that she had come home for a while. They turned to see all her possessions crammed into her little Honda and their hearts sank.

Never had a bird been so hard to push out of the nest as Darlene had been.

Still, she assured them she was only in town on assignment and would be going back to her job in the city. What Darlene didn't say was that she hoped to quickly transition to the West Ranch, and begin planning her grown up married life with Gunnar. She kept this secret to herself.

Reluctantly, Bud Shire and his wife, Mar, welcomed their daughter into the house once again, while shooting wide-eyed looks at each other behind her back. They had secrets too. They hadn't told her that as soon as she left for her job at the city paper, they repainted her room and turned it into a home gym, without an ounce of guilt.

"There's an inflatable bed in the closet," they told their nearly 38-year old daughter as she gazed in shock at her former walls, now lined with photos from her parents' travels.

Darlene's twin sister Daisy had been on her own since college.

Daisy parlayed her art degree into an internship, and then part ownership of Painted Bird Gallery, and was doing quite well for herself. They had a website and a blog, and sold original paintings and bronze sculptures to wealthy customers throughout the West, and beyond.

The more successful twin owned her own small house—one she was not willing to share with her sister, even for a few weeks. "Oh no," she told Darlene. "I shared a womb and then a room with you for far too long!"

The less successful twin only managed to turn her journalism degree into mounting credit card debt and an overstayed welcome in the Shire house.

"You don't stick to anything Dar," her father often scolded before she had left for the city. Her degree, he said, which he funded, was only the price of entry into the working world. "Now is the time to pay your dues and work hard to get ahead."

Instead, the Shires could only watch as their daughter half-heartedly attempted to make a name for herself. Too often they'd spot her car parked at one of the many taverns in town, or at Red's Rib Shack, instead of the local newspaper.

"I hate that paper," she'd lament. "They have me on the stupid obits."

And they did have her writing obituaries, until Darlene came into work with a hangover one day and filed a column for a local pastor that was riddled with mistakes.

Pastor Jim Bucknell stands before his great Cremator today. He leaves behind his wife and three grown children: one adult, and two adulteresses.

Somehow, amidst the errors, she managed to write a few lifestyle articles that got her noticed by the *Tri-City News* and they made her a job offer. Her parents thought it was unfortunate she had to leave Gunnar West, though.

Bud and Mar had begun to hope that if Darlene couldn't be successful, maybe she could be married. They started throwing money into a wedding fund, knowing that if their daughter married one of the Wests it would be a pricey event. When Darlene broke up with Gunnar and moved away, they spent the money on a Groupon trip to see the castles of Ireland.

She did look good in her new professional clothes, Bud and Mar thought, and hoped she had finally "found herself" in the city. What they didn't know was that Darlene didn't have a job in the city to go back to. She wasn't exactly let go, but her employment status had been "transitioned" to that of a freelancer.

"You have an opportunity to earn the same amount of money with pay-per-click articles," her editor told her with as much enthusiasm as she could muster, "but we can't keep you on the payroll any longer."

The Shires didn't know that Darlene didn't have any way to pay the credit card company, who wanted to be reimbursed for her new things at an interest rate of 25 percent, along with penalties and late fees. All they knew was that the morning after she arrived, she was up early, wearing a navy blazer and a yellow blouse. She was heading to the hospital to report on the quarantine.

"I'm stopping at the drug store for a few things," she said over her shoulder to Bud and Mar. "I'll put them on your account."

"Same old song," Bud mumbled to his wife over their coffee and toast.

CHAPTER 31

"Shoot," Kat whispered to herself, patting the pockets of her lab coat for the thermometer. It was early morning, and she told Josh she'd help with rounds and check the vitals of some who hadn't yet presented any symptoms of the virus. They were on the lookout for the warning sign of an elevated temperature.

Unless Ash lifted it with a sleight of hand trick, she knew she must have it in the lab, but didn't want to walk all the way back down three long hallways.

Kat arrived at the first semi-darkened room, which Gunnar slept in, and tiptoed to the side of the bed. His hat hung on a coat hook. His boots sat neatly on the floor.

Sitting silently on a stool next to the sleeping cowboy, she looked down at his still face. He was rugged, all right, and handsome. Though the light was dimmed, she could see that his complexion was ruddy but not flushed.

If he had the virus his breathing would be erratic, yet he was still and peaceful.

His strong arms lay at his sides and she could see the muscles and veins that traveled down from his broad shoulders to the backs of his hands—the hands that had unceremoniously helped her into his truck, tipped his hat to her, and wrapped fully around her waist when she was about to fall. The hands that brought her a ginger ale, and set up a midnight BBQ picnic— hands that pulled her effortlessly to her feet and brought her own hands to his lips.

Lips!

Kat recalled how her own mother took her temperature as a little girl, by placing a soft kiss on her forehead. Surely this sleeping cowboy wouldn't stir from a light brush—he wasn't a sensitive princess sleeping on top of a pea, after all.

Quietly and carefully, she bent down and placed a gentle kiss on his forehead. He felt cool and his skin was surprisingly soft. No fever, thankfully.

As she was about to stand up, one of Gunnar's hands flew up and wrapped gently but firmly around her wrist.

"Caught a snake," he said in a sleepy whisper, as he turned his head and squinted at her. There was a smile playing on the corners of his mouth, which made Kat smile in return.

"Sorry, not a snake," she whispered back, "just a doctor."

"What no-good trouble are you up to, sheriff?" Gunnar asked, now more awake.

"Just checking you for a fever, cowboy," Kat said.

"Is that so?" he said. "Don't we provide you doctors better equipment around here?"

"Yes, but my lips are pretty accurate," she said.

"So are mine," he said. And before she knew it, Gunnar slipped his arms around her and gently pulled her towards him. He was taking the lead but leaving room for her follow, if she chose to.

She chose to.

In the murky dawn of morning, their eyes found each other and held, and Kat exhaled with pleasure at the feeling of his strong, warm arms wrapped around her waist and back once again. As she leaned in, she could feel the heat radiating off of his skin—cool just moments ago, and now welcoming and warm.

"Kat," he managed, and then brought his lips to hers. With every exhale, Kat fell deeper and deeper into his arms and chest as he held her tight.

His kiss was firm and confident and she hoped it would never end.

At last, when she lifted her head, she searched his eyes once again.

"What brought that on?" Kat asked him.

"Our third date," he said, still holding her. "Isn't that the kissing date?"

"Third date?" Kat laughed softly. "What did I miss?"

She remained in his embrace, her face just inches from his own.

Gunnar told her that the first date was at the Italian restaurant, when, just as any gentleman would, he had helped her into his truck.

"*Helped* me—is that what you call it?" Kat laughed. "Okay, go on."

The second date, he said, was eating BBQ ribs on the floor of her hideaway.

"And the third?" she asked.

"Well, sheriff, I don't know how things go in the big city," he said, "but in these parts, when a woman is taking your temperature with her lips, I reckon that's considered a date."

Kat's pager began buzzing just then, and she stood up and stepped back from Gunnar. It wasn't easy—her legs trembled and she was unsure of her footing. She grabbed on to his hand to steady herself, and was amazed at how effortlessly her fingers entwined with his own. And how every nerve ending in her body was suddenly wide awake and expectant.

She hated to break away, because she wanted to know what he was thinking. The look on his face was unclear. If she had to guess, she'd say he looked surprised. As though he'd just discovered something monumentally important about the world that he never knew before.

Or maybe that's just how she alone felt.

KAT DIDN'T WANT TO ADMIT TO GUNNAR THAT HER EXPERIENCE WITH men was so spotty that she rarely had third dates. In her world of medical school, internships and a fast-paced career, the few men she'd gone out with remained on the back burner, and knew it. Still tingling from Gunnar's kiss, she felt quite accomplished all of a sudden—in just three days' time she'd gone from a disastrous blind date to a very successful third.

A full-blown relationship, she smiled to herself.

Thinking back a few days, Gunnar accused her of needing to trap a man in a quarantine just to hang onto him. At the time it felt like a slap in the face, but she hadn't had time to unpack the comment. Sure, she should be mad. But maybe there was a grain of truth.

Kat knew that of course she didn't create the virus, but was there really anything wrong with getting to know someone without thinking they were a flight risk? Couldn't a quarantine help them get beyond any awkwardness clumsiness—hers—and whatever reticence Gunnar had regarding commitment?

A disturbing thought creeped in. Maybe Kat could *only* hold onto a man under these circumstances. Maybe a quarantine still wouldn't be enough. Gunnar would leave at the first chance, Kat was sure. She had seen the trapped look in his eyes when she locked him in just days before, and the way he paced the hospital floor like a caged tiger.

The only reason he was flirting with her now, his captor, was to get on her good side. And maybe get an early release.

Gunnar would deny it, but people were complex.

She mentioned to him that the mind plays tricks. But was it okay as long as she knew the tricks and the inevitable outcome? She had warned Gunnar. They'd probably share a few innocent kisses in the next few days, just to break the tedium of the situation. Then, back in the real world, nothing more. They'd nod and smile when they passed on the street or in the hospital.

All would be forgotten... except the look in Gunnar West's eyes when he was inviting her, coaxing her into his embrace. Kat could never forget that. Or the feel of his warm and capable hands as he confidently held the small of her back.

Or the kiss that was unlike any she'd ever known.

It wasn't the clumsy kiss of a boy at a high school dance, or the rushed kiss of a fellow med school student celebrating a successful exam. It wasn't the polite kiss on the doorstep from a guy who was never going to call for a second date.

Gunnar kissed like a man who knew his place in the world, and he made Kat feel like an actual woman for the first time in her life. She wasn't just a doctor or the new girl in town—she was a woman who had kissed a man, and she'd never again settle for anything less.

Walking straighter and taller, Kat walked into a patient's room where she had been paged. Doctor Josh Quell looked up from the medical chart he wanted to show her and did a double take. Was it his imagination or did Doctor Tate look different somehow?

CHAPTER 32

The other person standing tall and straight that morning was Darlene Shire.

She felt good in her new navy blazer, the one she paid full price for. It would cost much more by the time she could pay off the credit card, she knew, but maybe Gunnar would pay it off for her once she had his ring on her finger.

Darlene was confident Gunnar would be happy to see her, and she knew no woman could have taken her place in the months she was away. First of all, Daisy would have told her. And second, Darlene knew every woman in town. There were no stones unturned.

Walking into the drugstore for her pricey face creams, the kind she could only have because her daddy owned the place, she felt excitement at the thought of heading to the quarantined hospital. Maybe she'd get a glimpse of Gunnar through a window, or the guarded doors.

But her happy bubble burst when she ran into Gunnar's friend, Jackie. Her instinct was to turn around and avoid her, but it was too late. Darlene braced herself.

"Darlene, is that you? I thought you left town!" Jackie was standing in the makeup aisle, wearing her scrubs. She had a small basket of items. Darlene couldn't help but notice that Jackie's greeting sounded more like an accusation.

I thought we got rid of you for good, is what Jackie probably wanted to say. Darlene knew for a fact that Jackie was relieved that she left town, freeing Gunnar to move on.

Darlene greeted her long-time acquaintance with pretend enthusiasm. Jackie, she knew, was protective of Gunnar and had cautioned him not to get serious with her.

"I'm back," Darlene said. "I'm about to head over to the hospital parking lot to cover the virus and the quarantine for the *Tri-City News*. I see you didn't get locked in."

"You reporters don't miss a thing," Jackie said with a plastered-on smile.

"No, we don't," Darlene volleyed back.

"Well, your old friend, Gunnar, is locked in," Jackie announced to Darlene.

"Really?" Darlene pretended this was news to her. "How did that happen, I wonder?"

It was common knowledge Gunnar West steered clear of the West Gorge Medical Center when he could, to avoid the unsettling memories of his mother's passing.

"It probably had something to do with that pretty young doctor," Jackie said, with a touch of mischief in her eyes.

"Oh?" Darlene fairly choked on Jackie's comment, in surprise.

"Kat Tate is the new infectious disease doctor. She's as pretty as the wildflowers that grow along the river," Jackie said. "I'm sure you'd just love her."

Already, Darlene definitely did *not* love Kat Tate, after just hearing her name spoken for the first time. She tried to remain cool and collected, but jealousy gripped her. Along with fear that her plan might not come together.

Darlene once had Gunnar in the palm of her hand before tossing him aside for her job. From the puppy-dog look on his face when she left, she just assumed he'd be waiting for her. Was she wrong? There was no love lost between she and Jackie, but could the nurse possibly be telling the truth about another woman—a doctor?

Jackie went on.

"Gunnar and Kat have been dating," she said. And with a conspiratorial wink, added, "I can't imagine what they were up to when they got locked in together, can you?"

Darlene regretted that her mouth dropped open in surprise, and wished she didn't give Jackie the satisfaction of looking shell-shocked. But she'd have the last laugh when she walked down the aisle towards Gunnar West, her soon-to-be fiancée.

Smiling, Darlene put her shoulders back and took her face creams to the register.

CHAPTER 33

"**P**raise the Lord," Marta said, handing Kat a paper plate with a chicken sandwich, chips and an apple on it. "Belle is recovering nicely and her surgical team has escaped the virus. June is doing well, too."

"That's a powerful prayer chain, Marta," Kat said.

"It is, Doctor Tate," Marta said. "Remember that if you need it someday."

Kat grabbed a bottle of cold iced tea from the refrigerator, and turned to go to her secret hiding spot to eat. A few minutes of peace and quiet would be a welcomed change from being pulled in a dozen directions, with very little sleep.

She was walking around the corner with her head down, thinking about asking the prayer chain to intercede on Ash's behalf—Kat genuinely worried about the boy and was sure Gunnar hadn't spoken to him yet about foster care. She hoped Gunnar wasn't too distracted with her to take care of his responsibilities.

"Whoa!" Kat looked up sharply to see she nearly plowed into Gunnar, who was walking towards her in the quiet hallway. His reflexes were fast and he caught her plate before her lunch landed on the floor.

"Why, sheriff," he said, "you're a million miles away."

"Guilty," Kat said, taking her plate back. "Care to join me for lunch?"

Gunnar nodded, and went to get a sandwich for himself. While Kat waited in the empty office, her heart raced at the thought of spending time with Gunnar West once again, and the butterflies in her stomach felt more like rocks tumbling around.

How did she ever think she could have a casual kissing relationship with Gunnar when she was so unnerved at the thought of being with him again? On one hand, she wanted to throw herself into his arms and enjoy the sensation of feeling safe and desired. On the other hand, she wasn't sure she could protect herself from getting hurt. Her heart seemed to be forging ahead—the one writing the check on the desert island.

Did it know what it was getting into?

Gunnar walked in quietly and pulled the door closed behind him. He stood there studying Kat and not saying a word, as she did the same. To his credit, he almost looked shy. That pleased Kat. He wasn't any more confident about where they stood than she was.

Finally, Gunnar placed a cushion on the floor for Kat and gently took her plate from her hands. He set it down next to the cushion, unfolded the napkin for her, and opened her tea. Then he gestured for her to sit.

"Ma'am," he said, taking her hand as she lowered herself.

"Thank you," Kat said in return. As she made herself comfortable, Gunnar sat opposite her with his own lunch."

They ate in silence for a few minutes before either spoke.

"You've been very honest with me, in a way I've never known before, Kat," Gunnar said in a low voice. "I have to say, you've caught me off guard a few times."

Kat looked up at Gunnar and waited for him to go on.

"I'd like to be just as honest with you," he said. "If you'll be patient, I can say my piece."

Kat quietly stopped eating and watched Gunnar's eyes as he spoke.

"I don't like this hospital and I avoid it when I can. It reminds me of my mother and the pain she suffered. Every wall here reminds me she's not in my life anymore."

Kat gently nodded.

"When the West Foundation donated the land and the funds to build this hospital," he continued, "it somehow felt like an offering to the gods of good health. Like, maybe nothing bad would ever happen to us Wests because we made this grand gesture."

Gunnar smiled a sad smile and hung his head for a moment.

"I know that's not how it works," he said.

Kat remained silent.

"Instead, it was just the opposite," Gunnar said. "My family sacrificed, and gave, and planned. Little did we know that we were building the place where the most precious person in my family would die."

Gunnar's jaw was clenched tight, and Kat could see the muscles working as he bit down hard. It reminded Kat of old Western movies, where a cowboy bit down on a stick to stop the pain from a gunshot.

At seeing his pain, tears welled up in Kat's eyes, which surprised her greatly. She could not remember the last time she shed tears—not even when her father left. Especially when he left. But now, it felt like her heart was constricting and squeezing tears right out of her, without her consent.

Gunnar was about to say more, but when he looked up and saw tears in Kat's eyes, he closed his mouth and fell silent. He was so moved by the doctor's compassion that he forgot, for a moment, the pain he himself had been feeling.

As their eyes searched each other's, they each found more than they had bargained for—new depths of feeling and a stirring of something much deeper than either had ever known. Something too powerful to be casual.

Could this be the real deal?

Reaching out, Gunnar took Kat's hand in his own and gently caressed her long fingers. She looked down in surprise and wonder at the intimacy of his hand holding hers. Even more than their electrifying kiss, this touch reached the very core of her being, and enveloped her soul in warmth and hope.

CHAPTER 34

"Oh, you know," Kat was saying to the reporter on the other end of the webcam and computer microphone, "we've had more than a few pizzas delivered, and no one turns down a late-night ice cream sundae when it presents itself. Once, we had ribs from Red's Rib Shack show up. Another night it was lasagna and garlic toast."

Kat scheduled her interview with the *Tri-City News* for late in the afternoon, when things were generally quiet in the wing. Shep told her that the reporter, whose name was Darlene Shire, was a feature writer and probably interested in what they ate during the quarantine.

Boy, had he called it.

At least Kat was safe from the questions that would catch her off guard, she thought.

"Close quarters for garlic toast, I imagine," Darlene said with a smile.

Kat nodded and smiled, reminding herself that this was a fluff piece and she could relax. And that was good, because her mind was far away, thinking about Gunnar West. They got close in a way Kat had never experienced before. She and Gunnar had gotten way past their disastrous first impressions of each other. They both shared deep feelings, from the heart, and knocked their first kiss out of the ballpark. Kat felt a shiver of delight at the memory.

Until Gunnar's disclosure about his painful loss, Kat assumed they would remain superficial to each other—a port in the storm to ride out the quarantine. But the opposite seemed to be true. The quarantine had put them on a fast track.

The cowboy and the sheriff.

The two of them might have some work to do when it came to dining out, but Kat would be happy eating picnics in the mountains and alongside the gorge with her handsome cowboy.

Kat smiled to think of what was ahead for she and Gunnar. The reporter probably thought she was smiling in response to her last comment—something about garlic toast. Kat knew she had to come back to the present and wrap up the interview.

Darlene, like everyone else, had questions about the virus itself. Kat went over all the symptoms, and gave her a tally of the number of sick and recovering patients. "It's mid-way through the week," Kat said, "and we have more people getting better than are contracting the virus, so that's very good."

Thankfully, the *Tri-City News* interview was winding down. Kat was tired, preoccupied from her lunch with Gunnar, and needed to check on her patients.

"Thank you for your time, Darlene," Kat said by way of ending the meeting.

"One more thing, Doctor," the reporter said, "I hear you have a VIP guest."

Kat thought for a minute, and drew a blank. Did she mean Belle? Kat wasn't about to trip over *that* line of questioning again!

"All our patients are VIPs, Darlene," Kat said with a smile. "So is our staff—everyone has been working tirelessly around the clock."

"I'm sure you're right, Doctor," Darlene said, "but I'm referring to Gunnar West himself—whose family foundation funded the hospital. It's interesting that such an important man should be locked inside his own building, don't you think?"

Kat squinted her eyes slightly as her assessment of Darlene came into sharper focus—who was she, really? And why did her questions about Gunnar suddenly make the hair on her arms stand up? Before she could answer Darlene's question, there was another one.

"Can you give Mr. West a message for me, Doctor Tate?" Darlene asked with an artificially sweet smile, before dropping her bomb.

"Tell Gunnar that his best girl is back in town," Darlene said. "Tell him I'm planning our wedding."

CHAPTER 35

*D*arlene eyed Kat Tate closely during the interview—trying to assess whether or not she was a serious rival for Gunnar's affection.

What did he find attractive? Darlene couldn't help but wonder.

She was pretty enough, though the doctor hadn't made any particular effort to look glamorous for the camera. Her hair was haphazardly piled on her head with a few unkempt ringlets framing her face. She wore oversized glasses that made her green eyes seem larger and greener than they were.

True, her complexion was fresh and enviable. Beneath the lab coat and scrubs, the doctor probably had a decent enough figure.

She was a few years younger than herself, Darlene surmised, but only a few.

If anything was going to intimidate Darlene, it would be Kat Tate's education, success, and the esteem she'd garnered through her research. Darlene's internet search turned up one of the papers Kat wrote for a medical journal, and she couldn't understand a fraction of what she was reading. She could barely comprehend the title: *Using Capture Analysis to Estimate blah blah blah Influenza-Associated Diagnoses...* or something like that.

It was definitely not written on a fourth-grade level, as Darlene's editor wanted her feature articles to be. It was no *Brunch on the Ranch*.

Still, Darlene felt a wave of insecurity, even as she enjoyed shocking the good doctor by telling her she was back to marry Gunnar West. Whatever hold Kat had on him, the cowboy was a man of integrity, Darlene knew. And while he hadn't exactly proposed to her, they both knew it was implied between them. A short six months couldn't change that, even if she had made it clear to Gunnar that she couldn't stay in West Gorge, or with him.

A girl could change her mind, couldn't she?

Maybe, but maybe not. Seeing Kat Tate for herself, and the way her face registered such raw pain that Gunnar was promised to someone else, shook Darlene's surety that he would still be hers for the taking.

CHAPTER 36

*A*sh Gibson cried himself to sleep most nights. Even now, sliding into his 16th birthday. It was the only way he knew to silence the voices in his head that told him he wasn't good enough for anyone to love, or keep.

Granny loved him.

In his earliest memories, she always remembered his birthdays and Christmas by sending him cute cards with puppies and spacemen on the front.

They were already opened when his mother would hand them to him. She said it was because she didn't want him to get a paper cut, but Ash figured out that she was taking the money. His mom was never smart enough to read the card itself, which often said things like "take the fifty dollars and buy what you want from Santa."

Santa never came to Ash's house. Nobody did. As a boy, Ash would sometimes ask his parents if he could invite a friend over after school, but they'd look at him and each other with such shock and surprise.

"Forget it," he'd say, and they did.

School was the only place Ash liked being. He always had a punch card that was good for a hot lunch—breakfast too, if he got there early enough. And the teachers liked him. He never caused trouble and he always had his homework done. What else was there to do at home?

Ash had just turned twelve when his parents surprised him after school by picking him up. "We're going to see Granny," they said, and he was happy about that. Although it seemed odd that it wasn't a holiday, or summer even.

It wasn't even a weekend.

Granny gave him a big hug and fussed over him like mad, even though he could tell she hadn't expected them. Once they thought he was asleep in the little room upstairs, Ash could hear the hushed angry voices of the adults, as their tones traveled through the grate in the floor where the heat came up.

"That boy deserves better than the likes of you two," Granny said.

"I reckon he does," his mother spat back at her.

In the morning, his parents were gone. Granny sat at the little kitchen table with a weak smile on her face and deep circles under her eyes. She told him his mom and dad would be gone for a spell, on a vacation. Ash knew they would never come back.

"Let's get you set up," she said, "just in case you stay here for a little bit."

Granny took him shopping in West Gorge. She bought him three pairs of jeans, five shirts, and new runners that didn't pinch his toes like the ones he'd been wearing for more than a year. "Throw those old things out," she told him, and he did.

She packed his lunch every day for school and when he came home, there was a roast in the oven, or a stew simmering. Ash had never known such aromas in his young life.

Everything was okay until about a year ago. When he walked into the little house after school, he could smell something burning. The roasting pan was in the oven, smoking, while the uncooked roast sat on the counter.

"Supper will be ready soon, Samuel," Granny called from her bedroom. Samuel, Ash knew, was the name of his grandfather who died many years before. One day shortly after that, he opened his lunch bag to find a can of butter beans from the pantry, and Granny's car keys.

Ash knew that there was no safety net for the two of them except for each other. He began taking her car to the store while she slept, using the back roads less traveled by the West Gorge police. Using her bank card, he would then buy frozen dinners and sandwich fixings.

He began intercepting the mail and paying the utilities with her check book. He'd open her bank statements each month and make sure to balance the accounts. But more and more, Ash felt he could not leave her for an entire school day. He understood that once Granny got the help she needed, nobody was going to let him drive her car or use her bank card for groceries. Or even stay in her house.

Ash knew he was going to have to fend for himself, and soon.

When he first saw the blue purse just sitting in the shopping cart, wide open with the wallet partially sticking out, he couldn't believe someone's carelessness. While the owner walked away to exchange the pancake syrup in her hand for a different kind, it was so easy to slip the wallet in his pocket, and then quickly finish his shopping and pay.

Out in the parking lot, Ash removed the cash—80 dollars—then dropped the wallet by the entrance where some upstanding citizen would inevitably hand it to the manager, who would find the owner.

"Goodness, I didn't realize it had fallen from my purse," she'd say, taking responsibility.

It was so easy finding cash in West Gorge. It was just right there, waiting for Ash; sitting in the open purses, the yard sale money boxes, and the "on your honor" deposit boxes for fresh eggs and firewood.

Ash was astounded that so many trusting people left wallets in inside pockets of their coats, or in their unlocked cars.

He didn't want to take money, but he honestly didn't know what other choice he would have once he could no longer take care of Granny. Soon, she would have to go into a hospital or nursing home. At least with the cash he had stuffed in a tin box, hidden in the shed, he'd be able to eat. And maybe find a place to stay for a while.

If he could survive on his own until he turned 16, maybe he could find work.

The quarantine was a game changer, Ash knew, and it wasn't all bad. There were wallets and purses everywhere in a hospital, which is why he came here in the first place. Grabbing a bouquet of flowers from a sleeping woman's room was a brilliant cover, if he did say so himself.

That is, until Doc Tate sniffed him out and made everyone lock up their valuables.

The big cowboy cramped his style at first too, but then he started to be useful to Ash, by teaching him how to play poker. That would come in handy someday. He didn't even mind helping the cowboy do stuff, like organize and clean the kitchen. Mostly because they would work together and that made it kind of fun.

There was unlimited food being delivered to the quarantined people, like he'd never known before. Pizza, tacos, ribs and lasagna. And women like Marta and June who couldn't feed him fast enough.

"We got to fatten you up, Ash," they'd say, and he'd let them. It was nice being mothered, and grand-mothered.

When they went about working on their scrapbooks, he created a hidden stash of granola bars, cereal boxes, and cookies for when he had to walk out the door. He almost had a nice watch, a stethoscope, and a few phones, too, until the nosey doctor discovered them.

Nosey or not, he had to tell Doc Tate about Granny so she would have someone look in on her. With him gone, she could burn the house down, or worse. But now, Doc had told him, Granny was under a doctor's care.

With the right medication, Granny could get better. She could go back to cooking the roasts and stews, and packing his lunch once again with sandwiches, instead of inedible items.

Maybe, Ash thought, he could go back to being just a kid again.

CHAPTER 37

Tell Gunnar that his best girl is back.

The words flooded Kat's mind.

His best girl was back! What did that make Kat? She already knew that answer. She was the girl that has to lock up a man to hold onto him.

"And even then, he gets away," Kat said out loud, despondently.

Kat thought she kept her cool when the reporter said she was Gunnar's best girl, but wasn't sure. That Darlene Shire was watching her reaction very closely, almost too closely to make any sense. How could she possibly know what's been going on inside the hospital walls, and specifically, behind closed doors?

Darlene could not be privy to the way Gunnar pulled her into his strong and lovely arms in the wee hours of the morning. The way he drew her deeper and deeper into his eyes, until they kissed. She could not know about the tears and the caresses they shared at midday, and how their hearts had moved one step closer to each other.

She didn't think Gunnar would kiss and tell. But a woman would not start planning a wedding unless there was a groom. *Was* he kissing and telling—were Gunnar and Darlene laughing at Kat behind her back, and playing her for the fool she obviously was?

Before she could check herself, Kat was full-blown mad.

Years of pent-up frustration and emotion worked its way up from her toes to the top of her head, like a boiling red thermometer in a childhood cartoon. She could almost feel the steam rising in her as she stomped down the hallway in a rage.

"Someone's gunnin' for bear," Gunnar said to himself when he saw her pass. He was tucked away in one of the small rooms on a phone call, and had no idea that he was the bear.

While Gunnar held the phone and waited on hold, he thought fondly of the spirited Kat. She was both the cause of this infernal lockdown and the only thing that made it okay.

He'd tasted a lot of kisses in his lifetime, but none that had unnerved him like Kat's kiss—none that he was still thinking about hours later. He was starting to anticipate a second kiss, and couldn't wait to get out of the hospital and take the beautiful doctor out for a real date. Maybe in a car this time, he thought. Although the memory of helping Kat into the tall truck would forever hold a special place in his heart.

He had to shake his head to clear the image of Kat in her little blue dress, and focus instead on how much he'd come to know and appreciate her honesty, her intelligence, and the way she took charge over impossible situations at the hospital.

Gunnar admired the doctor, but was starting to have real feelings for the woman. She was lonely in West Gorge, she told him, and he wanted to fix that. Just like repairing a broken piece of fencing on the ranch, Gunnar had a strong desire to shore up Kat's heart and make her happy any way he could. Somewhere inside of her was a sadness that went beyond loneliness. She'd tell him in due time, he was sure. As long as he proved to be someone she could trust. That's what he aimed to be for her.

"Gunnar, are you still there?" The voice on the phone brought him back from his thoughts. "Yep," he answered, "I'm still here."

. . .

As Gunnar continued his conversation, Kat had circled back down the hallway. Unable to find Gunnar to confront him about being engaged to the reporter, she took a deep breath and thought maybe it was good she hadn't. After all, they'd only shared one kiss and a rib dinner on a desert island. Nothing worth flying off the handle about.

She thought of her mother again and felt sympathy for the first time. Her parents were married nearly 20 years when her dad left—no wonder her mom had been hysterical.

"I've only known Gunnar for four days," she reminded herself.

Kat took another deep breath, and was heading to her patients' rooms again when she thought she heard Gunnar's voice coming from one of the small offices in the hallway. She walked quietly towards the sound. She could only hear his side of the conversation, but it told Kat everything she needed to know.

"Yes, ma'am," Gunnar was saying, "I do know it's a big step."

Kat's shoulders dropped in dismay. Was marrying Darlene the big step he referred to?

"I am ready for that level of commitment," Gunnar said. "And yes, the entire West family will be very supportive of this decision."

So, it's true, Kat thought. Gunnar is ready to commit and he and Darlene Shire will become engaged. His family couldn't be happier or more supportive. He used Kat to pass the time and she played right into it.

She should have known better.

Her heart squeezed just then, tightly. It was the same sensation she felt when Gunnar was telling her about his mother—the same sensation that made her cry for the first time in years. Decades.

But she willed away unbidden tears this time.

If she ever cried again, she promised herself, it wouldn't be over the likes of Gunnar West.

CHAPTER 38

"The worst is past, Shep," Kat assured her boss on the phone, to his relief. "The eye of the ResVi storm is behind us."

It was day five, and except for Belle Wild and her emergency surgery, the situation with the contagion had been textbook. They detected it early, and kept it from spreading through the community "like wildfire," as one of the quarantined had observed.

Most every patient was on the mend, and the few in the midst of the fever were expected to recover quickly. The mood was shifting from resignation to optimism as people got excited about going home.

"By the time we open the doors in a few days," Kat told Shep, "our patients will be fever-free and no longer contagious. Those that have stayed healthy are likely immune."

Shep Arndt had kept the detractors at bay, thanks to Kat and her positive talking points. And thanks to Gunnar and his first-hand account of all that went on behind the locked quarantine doors.

"Gunnar West tells me you're an ace specialist, Kat," Shep said. "He has every confidence in your abilities, as does every member of the hospital board. Well done."

"Thank you, Shep," Kat said, not wanting to hear Gunnar West's name any more than she had to. "It has been a team effort though, and

Josh Quell has certainly earned our gratitude—along with the nursing staff and the other doctors that stepped in."

"Humility," Shep said, "I like that, Kat. It's a sign of a true leader."

Whatever, Kat thought, only half-listening to Shep. She was weary to the bone. Weary to the heart and soul of all that was within her. He was saying that she should take some time off if she could, and recover at home. As soon as possible.

"You sound beat," Shep said. "I don't want my star doctor to get burnt out."

Kat nodded, though he could not see it over the phone.

"Good idea," she said. "I will take a little time off."

What she didn't say, but thought, was that she would use the time to update her CV and begin searching for another position, in another town. Maybe she could get out of Dodge before the big social event in West Gorge: the wedding of Gunnar and Darlene.

She just didn't think she had the stomach to watch the cowboy who had kissed her so convincingly marry another. Not when she had started to hope and believe that someday, it might just be she and Gunnar walking down the aisle—'til death parted them.

Death or abandonment.

"Cowboys and car salesmen," Kat said out loud with a sneer.

"Sorry, Kat—what was that?" Shep was still on the phone and she had forgotten.

"Oh..." Kat tried to recover. "A car salesman... I need to go car shopping."

They ended their phone call, and Kat dropped her head in her hands. *Cowboys and car salesmen. Men.* An untrustworthy lot, each and every one of them. They wooed your heart, they captured your heart, and then they broke your heart.

What was it about the Tate women that made men think they could take advantage? Women like Darlene, on the other hand, pretty in her blue blazer, could come and go as she pleased and command the world around her. Shep said she had local roots, but was from out of town.

"She snaps her fingers," Kat said to herself, "and cowboys come running."

One in particular. The best one.

Kat knew it was her own fault she was feeling battered and bruised. She knew the antics that went on when people were locked up together, isolated from their real lives and responsibilities. She knew better than to let her guard down and open up her heart.

She consoled herself thinking about how she and Gunnar West would be a disaster. Their blind date had proven that.

DOWN THE HALL, AT THE OTHER END OF THE WING, GUNNAR WEST WAS happier than he'd been in a very long time. Maybe ever. He had true challenges ahead of him, but had never shied away from those; all of a sudden he had a sense of hope about life, love and the future.

He also had what he considered to be good news and couldn't wait to share it with Kat. The last time he saw her she was stomping by the room where he was on a phone call. That had been a while, maybe an hour.

Gunnar set out to find her. She might be sleeping in the physician's lounge, or with a patient. Sometimes he passed a room and was comforted by the sound of her voice as she spoke with Josh Quell or a nurse. Other times she was talking with a patient, commiserating with their aches, pains and fevers. Or celebrating with them after their fever subsided.

The last place he went to look was her secret office, at the very end of the long quiet hallway. When he arrived, the door was closed and the room was silent. He knocked gently and when there was no answer, he slowly opened the door. Kat was sitting on the desk wearing fresh scrubs, holding her head in her hands so completely that he could not see her face.

"Kat?" he asked, tentatively.

Immediately, Kat removed her hands and stood up, away from Gunnar. Her face was hard and angry as she looked at him accusingly.

Gunnar's smile faded and his hands instinctively moved up to touch her. She flinched and moved a step back.

"I forgot that you own this hospital," Kat said in a cold, professional tone. "I suppose that's why you feel it's your right to open closed doors and ignore privacy."

His face reflected the shock he felt at her words and her rigid body language.

"What's going on? What happened, sheriff... Kat...?" Gunnar asked, helplessly. His hands moved once again to comfort her, but he stopped himself at the look in her eyes.

"It's Doctor Tate, to you," Kat said, walking out of the room.

CHAPTER 39

"*That* Jack Tate could sell ice to an Eskimo!" Jack's boss, Steve Vance, used to tell anyone who cared to listen. Vance put his full trust in Kat's father, who started as an assistant and became manager at Vance Auto Spot within a few years.

As the owner, Vance wanted to take the occasional long lunch, or maybe a vacation to Florida with his wife, but could only do that with the right people in place. In the year 1999, it looked as though he had succeeded.

The only flaw of Jack's that Steve Vance could detect was a stubborn unwillingness to get excited about the impending millennium, and ways to create a sense of urgency for car sales. He was one of the few people in the world not excited about the calendar changing over to 2000.

But that wasn't always the case.

Jack remembered being a boy in grade school when a teacher brought up the fact that most of his class would be alive when the calendar would change to 2000. The teacher had Jack and the other kids draw pictures of what they thought life would be like in 2000. And most every boy had drawn pictures depicting life in outer space.

Jack had forgotten all about that drawing, until the media's furor drew him back to his past hopes and dreams; the ones he'd long laid down.

As a boy, his futuristic rendering showed a happy stick family living in a rocket ship, wearing sleek silver body suits. As if the need for cotton, and pants with belts, would be obsolete in the next millennium. The students wrote out the math equation, and Jack knew he would be 39 in the year 2000—practically ancient.

Surely, he would have a family of his own, the young Jack figured. His sleek shimmery family that lived on the moon.

Jack himself would ride a rocket ship to work each day in the cosmos. He'd be a famous astronaut and explore the universe. And he'd come home every night to whatever dinner he wanted at the push of a button, and a robot dog—like the one George Jetson had.

Each night, the grown-up futuristic Jack would play with his silvery, shimmery son, who would be called Zip, or some other name that meant "fast." They'd play catch with an anti-gravity orb that glowed like it had stars surrounding it.

His shimmery wife would admire him.

Jack spent hours and hours as a boy, dreaming about how cool the future was going to be. But somewhere along the way it became ordinary.

"How is it that life fast forwards so quickly?" he once asked his boss, who only laughed and clapped Jack hard on the back.

"Quicker the better, son," Vance had said.

Jack's boss, he knew, was anxious to sell the dealership and take his early retirement in Florida. He had a house on the water waiting for him, and an RV to explore the world in.

But Jack didn't have anything ahead worth getting excited about. His best years were likely behind him. Here it was, the last few months of 1999, and Jack Tate was not an astronaut. Jack Tate was a used car salesman in Transom, Illinois.

Jack's wife, Trudy Tate, did not wear shimmery silver body suits. She wore oversized bulky sweaters and itchy wool skirts. After her long days at the public library, Trudy would come home and put fish sticks and little frozen potato nuggets in the oven, then help their daughter Kat with her homework. The two would sit on their brown sofa and pore over papers.

Kat was a good enough kid but she was quiet. She never wanted to play catch, even with a regular old ball. There was nothing he could see in his life that was shimmery or fun. Soon it would be a new millennium, and everything in Illinois and in Jack Tate's life would remain dry, dusty and brown.

It was as if the world was getting ready to shed its old skin and glow like a shining new planet, while he was doomed to be left behind in the dingy, dirty old world. Where his only high points being a trusting boss, frozen fish sticks, and the yearly corn festival held in a nearby town.

All that changed when Sugar MacDonald walked into the dealership and Vance sent her out to Jack's lot. "That tall good-looking man is going to take care of you, sweetie," he had said, and Sugar smiled. Her gaze followed Vance's arm to where Jack stood, laughing with one of the mechanics.

Mid laugh, Jack turned to see a vision walking his way and their eyes locked. Sugar had just turned 29 and wore a short shift dress the color of sunshine.

"I'm looking for something with a few miles, that still has a bright future. You know what I mean?" She held Jack's stare. "Dependable, but a little bit sexy."

Jack knew his mouth was hanging open, but couldn't help himself.

"Are we still talking about cars?" He asked her.

Sugar lifted one of her manicured hands to touch the sleeve of his suit coat. Jack was glad he'd worn his best that day.

"You're the salesman," she said, flashing a brilliant white smile. "Sell me."

Rallying, Jack put his hand under her bent elbow and guided her to a 1995 Ford Mustang convertible GT that had just come on the lot. He opened the driver side door and helped Sugar into the car. He got into the passenger seat.

They both put on their sunglasses and smiled at each other.

"When do we have to be back?" Sugar asked Jack as she turned the key.

"I don't have any reason to come back," he answered.

CHAPTER 40

G unnar's phone started blowing up with messages and texts that night.

"Since when are you and Dar back together?" read one from Pike.

"Dude, you're getting *married?*" read another from Colton.

He had no idea what was going on, until Jackie forwarded an article from the *Tri-City News*, digital edition. The headline made him choke on the apple he was eating:

Reporter Says "Yes" to Quarantined Cowboy

When Gunnar saw the reporter was none other than Darlene Shire, the blood drained from his head and he had to sit down. Reading the opening paragraph, he knew it was a good thing he was locked in the hospital, because every part of him wanted to go after her with a big truck and a mean dog.

He was livid.

Imagine my surprise at discovering that the man who asked this reporter to marry him was trapped in the quarantined West Gorge Medical Center; the story I was sent to cover. With the ghosts of his mother's death lurking everywhere inside those hospital walls,

Gunnar West, town philanthropist, needs a reason to hope—and that's where this reporter becomes the story: Yes, Gunnar West, I will marry you.

Reeling from the shocking words, Gunnar wanted to throw the phone against the wall. Instead, he turned it off and set it aside. He didn't trust himself with projectile objects.

He didn't know where to begin his damage control—he should call the hospital's PR team for a statement, and the press agent for the West Foundation. "Reports of Gunnar West's engagement to a reporter are greatly exaggerated," he would instruct them to say. Gunnar wanted to call his lawyer and sue both the paper and Darlene.

Ghosts of his mother's death... how dare Darlene bring his mother into her article?

And poor Kat!

This was the reason she was so hurt and so cold to him. Darlene was the reporter that interviewed her in the afternoon, obviously. What did she say to Kat, and how could she know the two of them were getting close?

Darlene turned her back on him and West Gorge. She had no reason to be back, unless she failed in the city and thought of Gunnar as her fallback. His friend, Jackie, warned him of such a possibility, but it didn't seem plausible until now.

Gunnar knew he needed to go find Kat and explain. But when he walked out of the little office, he heard crashing sounds and angry voices coming from the lobby—or perhaps it was just one sobbing and anguished voice. Quickly, he sprinted in that direction.

"Ash please! Let's talk about this," Gunnar could hear Kat pleading.

When Gunnar arrived, he saw Ash had picked up and thrown one of the lobby chairs against the wall, and then another. He held a third chair over his head as hot tears streamed down his red and blotchy face.

Marta, Josh, and a few of the others stood at the edge of the room with their mouths gaping, trying to avoid being caught in the line of fire. Kat was a few feet away from Ash trying to reason with him and calm him down. A security guard was quietly inching towards Ash with a live taser in his hand, Gunnar could see.

"My God, what's going on here?" Gunnar boomed, walking swiftly between Ash and the guard. He held his hand up imploringly, causing the guard to pause.

"Please," Gunnar said to the guard, "*please* let me handle this."

Everyone turned as a third chair crashed onto the floor of the room. It bounced off of a wooden side table, causing a lamp to fall and break into a dozen pieces. Ash turned then to Gunnar, racked with deep sobs. His shoulders sagged as he appeared to have used every ounce of strength and energy lifting and throwing the heavy chairs.

"I'm *not* going, Gunnar," Ash cried with hysteria in his voice. "I'm not going to a foster home. That's not how my life is going to play out. It's just not."

"Shh, shh," Gunnar tried to hush him as he walked slowly towards the boy. He had his hands out in front of him as if gentling a wild pony. "It's okay, Ash."

"It's not okay!" Ash sobbed again and shouted, but with exhaustion in his spent voice. And something else, Kat thought, moving closer as well.

"Yes, son," Gunnar said kindly. "It is okay."

He had almost reached Ash when the boy turned towards Kat and exclaimed, "*She* told me Granny was taken away and isn't coming back. And I'm going to a foster home."

Gunnar shot Kat an angry glance.

In return, she looked helplessly at Gunnar and whispered, "he had a right to know."

How the tides had turned, Kat thought. Just an hour ago, she had been so angry and Gunnar had been helpless. Now, she was the one completely without excuse. Had she taken out her frustration on this poor motherless child, when it was Gunnar she wanted to hurt?

Kat would never be able to forgive herself.

Gunnar took a step towards Ash. The boy let out a final sob while weakly swinging his fist to lay a blow. Instead, he fell into Gunnar's arms like a rag doll. Gunnar caught him in surprise, then immediately looked at Kat. The anger on his face turned to real fear.

"He's burning up," Gunnar said in alarm.

In a flash, Josh Quell grabbed the nearest wheelchair by the lobby entrance, and flew it over to where Gunner was holding Ash up with great effort. Together, they lowered the limp boy into the chair. Josh took over, running him to one of the open rooms for ResVi patients. Nurses followed behind, along with Kat and Gunnar.

With the boy passed out on the bed, Kat pulled out her stethoscope and listened to his heart and lungs. A nurse hooked him up to fluids through an IV, and Josh typed his name into the computer. Once he located his medical chart, he read it for pre-existing conditions that might complicate his treatment and recovery.

"Asthma," Josh said to Kat, soberly. They looked at each other with alarm. As if on cue, Ash started wheezing and breathing erratically. The nurse put an oxygen mask over his mouth.

"We have to get this fever down, fast," Kat said to her staff. To Gunnar, who was standing at the foot of Ash's bed, she said, "you'll have to leave the room. We will let you know when there's anything to know."

GUNNAR OPENED HIS MOUTH TO OBJECT. HE STILL WANTED TO BE ANGRY with Kat and knew she was still angry with him, but everything took a back burner to the boy's condition. Kat laid her hand gently on his arm and looked into his eyes. Her concern, he could see, mirrored his own. "It's okay, Gunnar, let us care for him. I'll find you."

Gunnar walked out into the lobby. He saw that Marta and the security guard had righted the furniture that Ash had thrown in his anguish and swept up the broken lamp shards. Other than a dent in the wall that would need repair there was no real harm done.

How lonely and scared the boy must be, Gunnar thought, sadly.

When Randi died, Gunnar wanted to do exactly as Ash had—throw large things and cry and rant. As if he could rip the great pain out from his grieving body by the handful and throw it far away from himself. He drove up to the mountains with his sleeping bag and there he stayed for a full day, crying into the heavens and throwing tree limbs and boulders. Anything he could find, until he was spent.

Eventually, he had to reappear for his mother's funeral. He needed to comfort his father and two brothers, and take comfort from.

Gunnar remembered the day he first saw Ash disrespecting Kat in the hospital lobby. He wanted to deck the kid—the way men answered problems in the west. But he also recognized something in Ash's eyes. It was the same pain Gunnar felt about losing his mother. Only, Gunnar had his father and his brothers. He had family and friends.

What if he had no one at all?

Gunnar couldn't imagine being alone in the world, as Ash was right now. His cowardly parents abandoned him and bolted to Mexico, and his granny suffered from dementia. She may know Ash when she saw him, and she may not. Either way, she could no longer take care of him. Though Gunnar suspected it was Ash who had been trying to care for her.

"Mr. West, can I get you anything while you wait?" It was Marta, heading to the break room after cleaning up the lobby.

"There's one thing you can do, Marta..." Gunnar started to say.

"He's already on the prayer chain, if that's what you want," Marta said. "Doctor Tate had us add him earlier. She's been so worried about him."

Gunner took this in and thanked Marta.

CHAPTER 41

*G*unnar awoke with a start in the lobby chair where he'd fallen asleep. Remembering where he was and why, he stretched his neck from side to side and frowned at the clock. It was three in the morning. His first thoughts were of Ash and Kat—two people he hadn't even known a week ago.

After washing his face, Gunnar made a fresh pot of coffee in the break room and carried two cups to Ash's room.

"Thought I'd find you here," he said quietly, handing a coffee to Kat. She was alone in the room except for a nurse, who turned to leave, and Ash. The boy was sleeping fitfully, his breathing labored.

"May I?" Gunnar asked, indicating a chair next to the one Kat was sitting on.

"Of course, Gunnar," she said, gratefully sipping the coffee. "It's been a long night, and far from over."

They glanced tentatively at each other in the dim light, searching for any traces of the hot anger they'd each felt just hours before. Neither found any.

"How is he, Kat?" Gunnar hoped she'd allow him to call her by her name once again.

"He's not good. The asthma is a worry," Kat said. "If I have to, I'll put him on a respirator. It's a last-ditch effort that could weaken him even more if his body rejects it."

Gunnar nodded solemnly.

"I'll contact West Gorge Human Services in a few hours," Kat said. "He doesn't have a guardian with his granny out of commission."

"Yes, he does. I'm his guardian," Gunnar said.

Kat looked at him in surprise.

"Are you referring to when I deputized you, Gunnar?" Kat asked. "This isn't the time for joking around. That was not binding."

Gunnar did not look like a man who was joking when he answered the doctor.

"I became his official guardian yesterday," Gunnar said. "I'm going to invite Ash to live at the ranch. We'll get him to school in town until he gets his license, and then he can drive himself. He can visit his granny every day if he wants, and we'll keep him busy enough on the ranch to work through his anger. In time, Ash will go to college—we'll see to that."

"Just like that?" Kat looked shocked.

"No, I've been working on this for a few days with Human Services," he said, "and it became official when I spoke to them yesterday. They wanted to make sure I was ready for the commitment, and that my family would be supportive. I am, and they are."

"Oh no... I believe I overheard that conversation, Gunnar, and I jumped to the wrong conclusions." Kat shook her head in despair.

"I was waiting to tell you and Ash until I knew for sure, but by then..." his words dropped off as they both thought of the events from the day before. Almost shyly, they ventured to look at each other.

"Gunnar..." Kat said.

"Kat..." Gunnar said at the same time.

"I thought you were so busy planning your wedding with Darlene Shire, that you forgot about the boy," Kat said in a whisper.

Gunnar looked miserable. They drank their coffee in silence.

"Did you ask Darlene to marry you, Gunnar?" Kat asked at last.

"No. Yes," he answered. "Not exactly. We were... starting to feel each other out on the topic when she up and left for a job in the city."

"She broke your heart," Kat said.

"That's just it," Gunnar insisted, "she didn't break my heart. I was relieved when she left because we would have made each other unhappy. Darlene is back because, to her, the grass always looks greener on the other side."

"I see," Kat said.

"She broke my trust though, by using my mother in her article. I don't ever want to see her again, or speak with her," Gunnar added. "And I'm sorry she drew you into her drama."

Kat nodded in silence.

"I broke your trust, too," Kat whispered. "I talked to Ash before you could. Also, I was pretty quick to believe Darlene Shire, without giving you a chance to explain."

Gunnar looked at Kat for a long time. She was such a tender-hearted person, and he found it impossible to believe she would ever mean any harm to Ash or himself, or anyone. He was not a fool—he knew the difference between mistakes and malice. And for such an intelligent, capable woman, Kat should know the difference, too.

Yet she spooked so easily.

"Who did it, Kat?" Gunnar asked, looking into her sad eyes, "Who broke *your* trust?"

CHAPTER 42

*J*osh Quell was in his late twenties and a full 10 years younger than his boss, Kat. But, as his own mother was fond of saying, "Josh was born at night, but not last night." He was quiet to the point of others not noticing him, which suited him just fine.

After finishing medical school and a three-year residency in internal medicine, the young doctor was happy to spend his time looking at germs and viruses under a microscope. He'd been told he had a bright career ahead of him, and silently agreed.

These were exciting days for infectious disease doctors.

With a decline in the vaccination rate, the oldie-but-goodies were coming back—measles, mumps and whooping cough, to name a few. And every year, new and dangerous bacteria, viruses and parasites emerged on the scene like ResVi and others; resistant strains of microorganisms that led to pandemics and epidemics.

Josh felt sorry for his med school buddies who had chosen safer, boring fields of expertise. Especially now, at the tail end of his first legit quarantine. He couldn't wait to begin writing the case study and could picture the glamorous headline:

ResVi Quarantine, West Gorge Medical Center, Wyoming

Doctor Tate might want to collaborate with him and that would be fine—unless she and the cowboy decided to kiss and make up. Then she might be otherwise occupied with matters of love. If they didn't make up, and remained star-crossed lovers, she might be too heart-broken to want to collaborate on the paper.

Either scenario was fine with Josh. He had nothing against love, and hoped to have a girl himself to kiss and make up with one of these days. Seeing Kat and Gunnar gave him hope.

As far as he could tell, the cowboy only had eyes for Kat. And it didn't take a microscope or a Mensa membership, both of which he had, to see that he had no intention of marrying the reporter who tossed her hat in the ring in such a garish manner.

Gunnar was not that kind of guy.

It also wasn't hard to see that on a cellular level, Kat had trust issues. Since she only ever talked about her mother in Illinois, and never mentioned her father, Josh could only surmise that her dad was the source of Kat's great pain.

From Josh's perspective, the two of them had made for great entertainment during the quarantine. He only wished Kat would confide in him so he could share his insights with her, and put her mind at ease a bit. Maybe that would come with time as they were both new to the town.

But Josh could only go so long without someone to talk with, especially under these confined circumstances. He was glad for his new friend, Marta, with whom he'd discussed all of his observations in the wee hours of morning.

They had a bet going. If Kat and Gunnar announced their engagement within six months, Josh would owe Marta five dollars. If they didn't, Marta would owe Josh.

It was a bet Josh fully intended on losing.

Either way, befriending Marta in the quarantine was the best thing that happened to Josh since moving to West Gorge. She was putting his name and his love life on the prayer chain, as an "unspoken" request. And to help God along, Marta said she knows half a dozen young women who would line up to meet the young doctor. Her own niece, Jaycee, included.

"She's a pretty little veterinarian and smart as a whip," Marta told him. "I'll have the two of you to dinner. Just don't bore her to tears talking 'bout germs all night honey, and you'll have a fighting chance."

CHAPTER 43

"I'll sit with him for a while, Doctor Tate," Josh said, walking in to Ash's room. "Get some sleep. Or at least some breakfast."

Kat nodded and slowly stood up.

Gunnar was gone. He went to find a shower and maybe sleep a bit more, she wasn't sure. He had given up on her after she wouldn't answer his question.

He wanted to know who had broken her trust.

Who *hadn't* broken her trust? That's what she wanted to shout at him. There were reporters with their softballs and blindsides, and her college friends and their exclusion. There was Gunnar himself, with his warm sweet kisses and a fiancée on the side.

But no. There was only one person who broke Kat's trust, and she thought she'd shut him out years ago when he left. Turns out, she'd been locked up with him all along.

Grabbing a fresh cup of coffee and a bagel, Kat made her way to her secret office. She'd eat in peace and maybe take a cat nap on the loveseat. Today would be pivotal for Ash's prognosis, and she would need her strength before the day was through.

The boy had mild hypoxemia—his nail beds had turned a worrisome tinge of blue. He wasn't getting enough oxygen into his blood and he needed to turn a corner, fast.

It was a good thing Ash was in the hospital when his symptoms reared their ugly head, Kat thought. His grandmother may not have had the presence of mind to call an ambulance.

Of course, he might not have been exposed in the first place if he'd stayed home, or stayed in school like he should have. Instead, he was off picking pockets in a hospital where a dangerous disease lurked. "Poor kid pocketed more than he bargained for," Kat thought to herself as she opened the door to her secret room.

Looking behind to make sure no one was in the hall, she slipped into her sanctuary, only to find Gunnar West sitting on the loveseat, quietly waiting for her.

Kat frowned in his direction.

"Don't you have a cake topper to pick out, or a tux to rent?" Kat asked him, but she was just picking a fight and stalling for time. She wasn't anxious to continue their conversation about hurts and betrayals—it demanded more than she had in her, here at the end of a tiring week.

But apparently, like Gunnar, the topic wasn't going away.

Gunnar ignored her jab. He patiently watched and waited while she exhaled in defeat, then reluctantly settled in on top of the desk with her breakfast.

Kat thought about the first night they met, and how he'd accused her of wanting to lock a man up and hold him captive to keep him from walking out. He had no idea how those words had resonated to the point of unravelling something inside of her. Something she thought she held pretty tightly until she met Gunnar.

Like it or not, Kat knew she had to face her father's abandonment and how it continued to affect her view of men. And maybe it was time to start talking.

After taking a sip of her coffee, Kat found Gunnar's eyes.

"He left my mom when I was 14, and about to head into high school," Kat said. "Dad sold cars for a living. He found a new passenger one day, and off they went into the sunset. I'm sure they are living happily ever after, wherever they are."

Gunnar sat forward and hung on every word as she spoke.

"That's really all there is to say about that, Gunnar," she said with a shrug. "He left my mamma, and she was a broken mess. Still is."

"He left you too, Kat," Gunnar said softly.

Kat shrugged again.

"I'm not the one who chased him to the car, sobbing and clawing," she said. "I'm not the one who ran half way down the street calling his name, while the neighbors all gawked from their front porches. That was all her."

Kat could see Gunnar swallow hard.

When he could speak, he said, "I'm going to say it again, Kat. He left you too."

Kat studied him, thoughtfully.

"Maybe we both left her," she said at last. "I couldn't wait to leave every morning for school, just to escape the weeping and the depression. I joined every after-school club there was. When there wasn't a meeting, I'd head home to my room and stick my nose in a book."

"You must have been crushed," Gunnar said.

"Her pain was sufficient for the both of us," Kat said, cavalierly. "I let her carry the burden of the suffering while I set about building a life where I would be independent and financially solvent. Never depending on anyone."

"Not a man who could walk out anytime," Gunnar said.

"That's right," Kat said. She was aware Gunnar would be leaving the next day, just as soon as the doors opened. He'd only be back for Ash, if the boy made it through the day. She cringed at the thought of Ash taking a turn for the worse. And she was sad at the turn her budding romance with Gunnar had taken.

Still, Kat longed for love.

"Gunnar," Kat asked him suddenly, looking at his dark eyes through the pain in her own, "what makes men stay?"

"They stay because they promise to, and want to," he answered too quickly.

"Until they don't want to," she said, irritated and unconvinced.

GUNNAR FELT A FISSURE IN HIS HEART AT KAT'S BROKENNESS—IT WAS AS real as the West Gorge that held the mighty river. He wanted to scoop her up and take her home, and spend the rest of his life proving to her that he was worthy of her trust.

He could tell her that he would never make her cry or run after him in agony, but would she believe him?

She was beginning to let her guard down until that snake, Darlene Shire, came back on the scene and rattled her to her core with talk of her wedding with Gunnar. Now, he honestly didn't know if he could win Kat back.

He was silent, then, thinking of Darlene. Gunnar had stayed with her, but just barely. The two of them could never seem to get past the fighting.

Sure, Ridge and Randi had an occasional argument, but the lion's share of their time was filled with love and whispers, dancing by the firelight and turning in early. Their lives were marked by commitment, and to things greater than themselves—to their family and community.

"Not all men walk out, Kat," Gunnar said at last.

"Not all women get sick, Gunnar."

KAT SURPRISED EVEN HERSELF WITH HER AUDACITY. AS A FIERY HOT anger rose in Gunnar's eyes, she continued.

"You want to fix me, but I believe you're messed up, too," Kat said. She knew he was fighting mad at her words, but there was no turning back now. "You avoid love to avoid pain. But you just trade one pain for another—you choose loneliness over loss."

Bullseye.

Kat could see she'd hit him hard, right where it hurts. In the truth.

"Darlene is out there planning your wedding, Gunnar," Kat said, standing up, "maybe you should show up for once."

An agonizing silence hung between them. Enough had been said. Maybe more than could ever be forgotten or forgiven. The only thing left to do, she thought, was to walk out, and close the door on what might have been.

As they got up to leave, Kat received a text from Josh Quell: *Come to 102 STAT.*

"Ash's room," Kat said in alarm.

CHAPTER 44

*D*riving out to the West Ranch was a risk, but one Darlene Shire was ready to take.

"In for a penny, in for a pound," she said to herself as her little Honda sputtered along on the ranch road. She hoped Gunnar would buy her a nicer car once they were officially engaged.

"Mrs. West wants a Land Rover, or a Cadillac," she told Daisy over a glass of wine at the little gallery the night before. Her sister gave her a smile that irritated Darlene—she knew when Daisy was humoring her. She was her twin, after all.

The fact that Gunnar hadn't called didn't discourage her—she was of the philosophy that if you just plowed ahead, people would eventually get with the program. A few years ago, Gunnar hadn't even known the two of them were dating until it became assumed by everyone in town, and reinforced by Darlene.

"I guess we're an item," Gunnar said one day, sounding more resigned than happy.

"About time you figured it out," she responded.

Her parents would get with her program, too. Darlene knew they weren't thrilled to see her come back, but she would simply move in and make herself at home again, until they told her otherwise.

Of course, the fact that they turned her room into a gym was a snag.

Sleeping on an air mattress was hard enough. But waking up on an air mattress in the dark of morning, while her mother ran on a treadmill in the same room, watching the home and garden network on a very loud TV, was another matter altogether.

Still, when it came to marrying Gunnar, she would proceed like it was a done deal. It nearly was before she left town, Darlene figured, and she'd only been gone six months. What could possibly have come between she and Gunnar in that short amount of time? Certainly not that little slip of a doctor—the one who had locked him in with memories of his mama. *He will resent her forever.*

The ranch cook opened the front door and reluctantly welcomed her inside.

"Miss Darlene," the old fellow said, nervously, "nobody's here. Were you expected?"

"Pretty much," Darlene said with a smile, as she stood on the cool tiled entryway with the massive antler chandelier hanging over her head. "I think you'll be seeing more of me in the near future, uh...." Darlene stammered as she tried to remember the cook's name.

He didn't help her at all.

"Oh, okay," Justice said with a lukewarm smile, "you must be helping with the child."

"Child?" Darlene said.

"I'm just in the kitchen, cooking for Gunnar's boy," Justice said, turning away. "You're welcome to wait there with me. Mr. Ridge or Mr. Pike might be home soon."

"Gunnar's boy?" She could hear the hysteria in her own voice.

The cook kept walking, which irritated Darlene.

"Who is Gunnar's boy?" She asked again once they reached the massive ranch kitchen.

"Oh, you know," Justice said, "his boy. The young boy who's coming to live at the ranch—right inside the house, with Gunnar and all of the Wests. Just like family."

Darlene stood shocked, with her mouth hanging open.

"He's bound to be hungry," he said, "and I'm not sure what all he likes."

Darlene looked around and saw that the old cook was making BBQ brisket, pans of lasagna, meatballs, cobblers, green beans and slaw. Pans of baked beans, roasted chicken and mac and cheese sat next to each other on the granite slab counters.

"I hear tell the child has been sick, so we need to build up his strength," Justice said, not really looking at Darlene, who was ashen.

He ignored her presence as she scrambled to think of who Gunnar's boy might be. She had only been gone for six months, so it couldn't be a baby.

Or could it?

Had he been untrue to her during their two rocky years?

Heaven knows, they fought enough during their off-again, on-again time together, and many nights, Darlene didn't see hide nor hair of Gunnar West. He would regularly stomp off or ride away in his truck. Other times he disappeared on horseback for days at a time. But Darlene always assumed he was alone.

She wasn't always alone, but figured he was.

Was "the child" Gunnar's from a previous relationship? He dated many women in West Gorge over the years. It could it be that Gunnar had a son he was just now finding out about. Maybe the mother had become ill and left her son… their son… to Gunnar!

"I reckon not *every* stone was left unturned," Darlene said under her breath.

Had there been a paternity test?

She desperately wanted more information, but could tell that the old cook was not going to disclose the details she needed to hear. Darlene's mind swirled with thoughts of a small child coming into the West Ranch.

"That would ruin everything," Darlene said to herself.

If the boy's mother was alive, Gunnar would feel loyal to her. If she wasn't alive, Gunnar would undoubtedly focus all his attention on the boy. And where would that leave Darlene? Being a free nanny and chauffeur, and playing second fiddle to some snotty nosed toddler.

A sickly child at that.

There was no way the Wests would use her like that, she thought angrily, as she grabbed her purse and turned to leave.

Darlene was resigned to the fact that someday she would have to pretend to love her own kid. She'd be expected to produce a West heir, she knew. But it made her livid to think some other woman had beaten her to it. Now, her poor child would never be the firstborn of the next generation of Wests.

What was the point?

CHAPTER 45

"Kid, you gave us a scare," Gunnar said to Ash. The young man lay weak and pale in the hospital bed, with a low-grade fever. His breathing had returned to normal, except for an occasional wheeze. The day before, when Josh sent a text to Kat, she and Gunnar came running to the room to find Josh wearing a broad smile.

"He's going to make it," he told them both, and the three of them hugged and laughed with relief. Ash took in the little group and then closed his eyes and fell into a deep, restorative sleep.

By that evening, Gunnar was able to talk to a weakened Ash and lay out his plan. The boy pretended he needed time to think it over, but it was obvious that he and the cowboy had bonded. Ash agreed to give it a try.

"Can I learn how to ride a horse?" Ash asked Gunnar.

"You'll ride a horse, drive a jeep, rope a steer and fix a fence—all before school every morning," Gunnar said with a slight smile. "Everyone pulls their weight at West Ranch. There's no free ride. You'll have me and Ridge, Pike and Colton, all in your business every day, son. So, rest up while you can."

Gunnar made like he was going to slap Ash on the leg, but pulled back and smiled.

The boy laughed weakly, then closed his eyes again.

Ash would remain in the hospital for another day or so, Josh told Gunnar, for observation. The West Ranch was a long drive from the hospital, and Josh wanted to be certain that Ash wouldn't have a recurrence of symptoms.

THE NEXT MORNING, THE DOORS FINALLY OPENED AND PEOPLE BEGAN walking out and straggling home—one after the other. Kat and her team scrambled to fill out exit paperwork. They had all been locked in for a week, but it seemed like a lifetime.

Gunnar wasn't a patient, so he didn't need to be out-processed. Kat was sure he was long gone. The first out the door.

Of course, he'd be back for Ash.

Kat thought back to Ash's miraculous recovery the day before. Josh texted her to rush to the boy's bedside, and since she was with Gunnar at the time, they held hands and dashed to his room—expecting the worst. Instead, Ash's fever had subsided.

They had all hugged and cheered.

Gunnar had reflexively squeezed her tight and she returned the embrace, longing to linger. But it was just relief they felt, she understood. Sadly, Kat knew that was the last intimate moment she'd ever have with him.

The quarantined cowboy was free to go.

Gunnar couldn't wait to climb in his big truck and hit the open road, she knew. He'd probably drive up to the mountains and hike along the gorge—just to confirm that he was blessedly free from restraints of any kind. Especially her.

Maybe Darlene had been waiting for him in the parking lot, like Nels, and other family members of people who were locked in. Kat couldn't bear to even glance at the touching reunion scenes being played out.

There would be nobody waiting for her, unless she counted the news cameras. The last faces Kat wanted to see belonged to reporters.

Kat knew she could drive herself crazy thinking about Gunnar with Darlene, and Gunnar with his freedom. She wanted to compartmentalize the cowboy, just as she had with her father. But it wouldn't be easy. Gunnar had pried open some long-closed doors and she doubted she could get them shut again on her own.

CHAPTER 46

"The doors are wide open Gunnar, just walk out."

This is what Kat planned on telling Gunnar when he came to say goodbye before leaving the hospital, but he simply left without farewells or fanfare.

Two days later, Josh discharged Ash. Kat's nerves were jumbled at the thought of Gunnar coming to see her when he picked the boy up. She looked out the hospital window and felt lightheaded at seeing his truck parked outside. Kat nervously pretended to be busy in her office as she waiting for him, but he didn't come.

Finally, she looked out the window again and the truck was gone.

And now, a month after the quarantine had been lifted, Gunnar West seemed out of Kat's life altogether. She hoped to never see him again.

The first few days, Kat didn't care about anything but sleeping in her own bed, and taking long hot baths in the soaker tub overlooking the mountains. She took walks near the gorge, wrote a long letter to her mother, and ate.

"Let me send you some ribs and slaw," Jackie called to offer. Her co-worker had heard about Kat and Gunnar's ill-fated blind date and wanted to make amends. "I'll add a few slices of my pecan pie—that cures everything," Jackie said.

"Maybe another day," Kat told her, sincerely. As much as she loved Red's ribs, they made Kat think of her picnic with Gunnar during their quarantine. And she was trying hard to forget the moments with him that threatened to crush her.

Six weeks after the quarantine was lifted, Kat finally ventured into downtown West Gorge to do some shopping. She bought jeans and shirts at the outfitters. "If you can't beat 'em, join 'em," she told the confused cashier.

Afterward, Kat browsed the bookstore. She chose a coffee table book with beautiful images of paintings by Western artist Frederic Remington, and loaded her purchases in a new Jeep.

She was about to head home when she noticed Painted Bird art gallery across the street. Kat had wanted to pop in and today would be a good day. The hospital board was holding its monthly meeting, so she felt safe being in town without any chance of bumping into Gunnar West—it was the only day she had the courage. On any other day, the safest place to be was the hospital itself. The last place he would want to be.

Kat fully planned on tending her resignation and moving on after the epidemic, but after a few nights' sleep she thought better of it. There was so much to be done in West Gorge. After realizing how unprepared they had been, Shep wanted her to develop new hospital and community protocols. He helped her connect with a Wyoming coalition of medical professionals doing the same thing.

She began meeting with community leaders to help educate citizens on ways to avoid contracting and spreading viruses of all kinds. Unlike her work in Chicago, which remained faceless for the most part, she was becoming attached to the people of West Gorge, and sincerely longed to keep them in good health.

Kat received a commendation from the CDC for her quick actions, but refused to speak to reporters. She left the press to the PR team at the hospital. But she did enjoy speaking to civic groups and school assemblies.

Marta and June, who became local celebrities after the quarantine, organized a wellness event at their church and Kat agreed to be the keynote speaker. The town's retailers asked her to attend their quarterly luncheon.

Her schedule would be full come Fall, if she stayed.

For now, Kat decided, she wouldn't let a failed romance send her running away from this wonderful town and its people. She couldn't hide from Gunnar forever, she knew, but she could get stronger before she saw him again.

To that end, Kat had been meeting with a colleague at the hospital —a therapist—who was helping her face her father's abandonment so she could acknowledge the pain once and for all.

"He left you too, Kat," Gunnar had said more than once. He was right.

As Kat locked her Jeep and walked towards Painted Bird, she thought of how much work was ahead, convincing store owners to add hand sanitizer to their entrances and disinfect surfaces. Maybe they could offer masks to customers who coughed or sneezed.

The window of the gallery had a revolving display of oil paintings and sculptures that always drew Kat's eye. It could be time to purchase her first original piece of art. The retail group might be more open to her input if she shopped local, and had a vested interest in their success. Today was a good start.

"Be right there," a woman's voice called out from a back room of the gallery.

"Take your time," Kat said back to her. She sat down in the center of the room on a teak bench, and gazed in admiration at a wall of oil paintings depicting the gorge in all seasons.

"That little winter scene is my favorite," the woman's voice said as she entered the room, behind where Kat was sitting.

"I love that one, too," Kat said, turning around. At seeing the saleswoman, Kat's mouth fell open and the color drained from her face. It was a terrible mistake coming here.

"*Dar...* Darlene!" Kat said in alarm, as the woman looked on with concern.

"Are you all right, ma'am?"

It was Darlene's face looking at her, but not her voice. Something was off, Kat thought as she felt her head spinning. She groped for the handles of her purse and grabbed on. All she needed to do was find her legs and she could run out of the gallery.

"I'm *Daisy*, Daisy Shire," the woman said. "Darlene is my sister— my twin, actually. People confuse us all the time."

Daisy got Kat a drink of water and sat down with her on the teak bench.

Ignoring Kat's erratic breathing and emotional response, Daisy pointed to a few of the paintings and gently began talking about the artists. Before long, Kat's heart rate stabilized and she found herself nodding at Daisy's rhythmic voice and wealth of knowledge.

"Now, Chaz Nash painted these smaller oils. He's a fine arts graduate from University of Oregon. Unlike the more detailed water colors next to them, the impressionistic oils are meant to be viewed from a distance," Daisy told her. "Nash is undiscovered, but has a bright future, I believe."

Daisy Shire was quite passionate about the artists she represented, and candid about the marketable value of the paintings. She steered Kat away from artists becoming too "saturated" in the market for their paintings to increase in value.

Nearly an hour later, Kat stood at the counter as Daisy wrapped up the little winter scene in bubble wrap and brown paper, and took Kat's credit card. It was a big investment, but one Kat was happy to make.

"Here you go, Doctor Tate," Daisy said with a smile, handing her the package. "I'll be sure to send you news about our upcoming gallery events, including wine and cheese socials with the artists themselves. It's a great way to dial in to the community. We're glad you're here."

Kat thanked Daisy, who said, "by the way, my sister left town weeks ago."

"Oh?" was all Kat could manage to choke out.

"She took a job with a gossip magazine in California," Daisy said with a sympathetic smile. "So, if you see anyone in town who looks like me… it will most likely be me."

CHAPTER 47

"I'm not taking no for an answer, Kat," Jackie said on the phone. "Today is the day."

It was the following Saturday afternoon, and Kat was cleaning the vegetables she'd purchased at the farmer's market. She could hardly wait to make a quiche with the leeks, and snap the green beans to throw in a simmering pot. Maybe she'd invite her landlord, JaneAnn, for supper.

"Jackie, I..." Kat tried to protest, but also didn't want to hurt her friend's feelings.

"Kat Tate," Jackie said in a no-nonsense voice, "I am too busy today to argue with the stubborn likes of you. I have a full rack of ribs and all the sides packaged up with your name on it. It's going to be delivered to #22 in about ten minutes—so I suggest you put some clothes on and get ready to answer the door."

Kat laughed hard at her friend's monologue, and that alone felt good.

"I gladly surrender," Kat said, "and thank you from the bottom of my hungry heart. I can hardly wait to taste those delectable ribs once again."

"You're welcome, girl. Now wash your face and put on a little lipstick," Jackie said. "We've got a mighty cute delivery man working for us today."

Kat smiled as she hung up the phone. The quiche would have to wait.

She thought Jackie was joking about gussying up for the delivery guy, but went to change anyway. The late August sun was warm as the day progressed, and the sweatshirt she wore to the market earlier was one layer too many.

Throwing on a crisp clean sundress, Kat ran a brush through her hair and applied a light gloss to her lips just as the doorbell rang.

Delivery *man* was right, Kat thought. He stood tall, and the box of food blocked his face—until he lowered it slightly. Then she could see who it was.

"Gunnar!" Kat said in surprise.

"Hello, Kat," he said softly.

Upon hearing his voice and seeing his dark blue eyes again, Kat's heart began pounding. She was sure Gunnar could hear it beating like a drum in a marching band, and she reached for the doorframe to steady herself. The two stood still until Gunnar broke the ice.

"Can I come in and set this down?" he asked her. "It's a little hot."

"Oh, sure," she said, scrambling to gather her thoughts.

Why was Gunnar West here?

He set the delivery box on her granite island, and started unpacking the containers. Kat could see that his hands trembled slightly, and realized he was nervous. She was too.

"Are you… hungry?" she asked, gesturing to the food, and he shook his head no.

Gunnar looked around the room. "This is a really nice place, Kat," he said.

"Thanks to the hospital board," she said, "which includes you, I suppose."

"You are an important addition to the community," Gunnar said, a bit awkwardly, Kat thought. She allowed herself to remember a time not so long ago when she believed she was important to Gunnar. She had a long way to go if she was going to get over him. Her legs felt weak just standing in the same room with him.

"I'm glad to be important… to the community," she said at last.

Gunnar was looking around like a caged tiger, Kat thought, and probably eyeing the door. But he surprised her.

"You look very pretty," Gunnar said.

Kat swallowed hard.

"Could we sit down for a few minutes, Kat?" he asked. "I haven't seen you in a while."

Kat poured them both a sparkling water with a slice of lime, and indicated the sofa. He removed his hat, and took a sip before setting his water on the table in front of them. Nervously, he picked up the binoculars, then set them back down.

"The view of the gorge is spectacular," Kat told him. "I wake up early every morning so I can watch the mountains come into view, and see the animals come to life. There's an eagle's nest in a pine nearby, and the mama is busy feeding the hatchlings."

She heard her own voice and felt like she was rambling, but wasn't sure what else to do.

Instead of following her gaze, Gunnar watched her closely. It made her uncomfortable, and more than a little bit sad.

"How's Ash?" Kat asked him.

Gunnar smiled at the question.

"Ash is doing well," he said. "Really good. He's working hard on the ranch, and my brothers are falling over themselves to bring him into the fold. We have a ranch cook named Justice, and he's made it his mission to fatten Ash up."

Kat smiled at that image.

"I'm happy for him. How's his granny?" Kat wanted to know.

"She's comfortable and well cared for—she has good days," Gunnar said.

They were quiet again. The topic of Ash had run its course.

"Why did you come here, Gunnar?" Kat asked in her softest voice.

At that, he shook his head a little and looked out the window.

"I didn't like the way things ended between us," he said.

Kat didn't either. The two of them had touched each other's hearts in a very short window of time—then slammed the window closed altogether with hurtful accusations and unresolved anger. But if her therapy had taught her anything, it was the importance of speaking up and putting her feelings on the table. Bottling things up only magnified pain.

"I don't suppose…" Kat started to speak but lost her nerve.

"What, Kat?" Gunnar asked, seemingly glad for a break in the silence.

Did she just imagine she heard *hope* in his voice?

"I don't suppose we can start over, Gunnar, as if the quarantine never happened?"

Gunnar took his time before answering.

"Start over? What would that even look like?" he asked.

"Well," Kat said, "if we pretended to meet for the first time, maybe we could be more open-minded about the other, and not so quick to judge."

"You and I were pretty quick to judge, that's for sure," he said.

Kat nodded her agreement.

"I think both of us could stand to be more honest about our true selves," Kat said.

"Honest, huh?" he asked her with half a smile. "Give me a sample of that."

Kat thought about it for a minute.

"I could say, *my name is Kat,* and I'm a disease doctor. I'm a fatherless girl with trust issues that manifest in unbecoming ways, like wanting to lock a good man up so he can get to know me," she said. "I like ribs, pizza, and long romantic walks in a quarantined hospital."

Gunnar nodded his approval. "That's a lot of honesty," he said.

"You?" She asked.

He took his time answering her, to the point where Kat thought he might not play along at all. She was wondering if she'd stuck her neck out too far, but then he began talking.

"I'd say what I should have said when we first met, that you are the prettiest darn thing I've ever laid eyes on. And I do not deserve to be in the same room with your kind heart and gentleness."

Gunnar and Kat looked at each other with sadness in their smiles.

They could not pretend the quarantine never happened—they'd come too far and learned too much. And though his rejection would be painful, Kat knew she had to risk everything, or regret losing the cowboy for the rest of her life.

"Do you think it would be possible," she asked him, "to re-do our first date?"

Gunnar sat forward and looked at Kat. She was beginning to feel uneasy, and braced herself for the bad news that it was too late for the two of them. When he finally spoke, she heard her worst fears coming true.

"No," he said at last, "I'm sorry, but no."

Kat nodded sadly and bowed her head. She wished he'd just leave, instead of sitting on her sofa, breaking her heart all over again.

"You see, Kat," he said, "I was hoping that I've had my last first date, and just maybe, you have too."

Kat lifted her head slowly, trying to make sense of his words.

"As awkward as it was, our first date was the beginning of our story," Gunnar continued, as a slow smile spread on his face. "And I hope to tell our children someday about how their mother wore an itty-bitty dress, then got stuck trying to hoist herself into my truck."

Gunnar wasn't rejecting her—just the opposite, Kat realized. He was talking about her as if he wanted her to become his... did he just say *our* children?

"They will tell that story at our 30th anniversary party Kat, and our 40th and 50th," Gunnar said, "you and I will be there to laugh and cry alongside them. Holding hands, just like this."

She looked over to see his hand waiting for hers.

Kat was still speechless as she placed her shaking hand in his.

"What do you say, sheriff," Gunnar said as he pulled her into his arms, where she'd longed to be since their first date, "are you ready to let me love you?" At that, Gunnar wrapped his arms fully around her and pulled her so tightly into him that she exhaled a cry in surprise and delight.

"Yes, cowboy," she whispered through a trembling voice. "I'm ready."

Leaning closer, he kissed away a tear that was falling down her cheek. Then he kissed away another and another... tenderly working his kisses towards her waiting lips.

CHAPTER 48

$\mathcal{A}$sh never worked so hard as in the four months since moving to West Ranch. Gunnar wasn't joking about chores—Ash was up before the sun, feeding livestock and fixing fences. Then he'd shower and ride into town with Kat. He could walk to school from the hospital.

Half way through the day, Ash would eat the massive lunch packed for him by Justice, the ranch cook. Usually it was built around a roast beef sandwich made on thick sliced bread.

After school, he'd walk to the West Gorge Nursing Home and sit with Granny while doing his homework. She didn't always know him and it was sad, but it didn't deter Ash from visiting her. She was still the only person who ever truly loved him, and gave him a real home.

Until the West family, that is.

He'd catch a ride home to the ranch with Kat, when possible. Other days, one of the Wests came to fetch him from town. Either way, the Wests were all in his business before and after school—each person more than the next. But he didn't mind.

"Show me your homework, Ash," Kat would say, until he relented.

"Tell me what you're learning, Ash," Ridge wanted to know, and no one said no to Ridge.

"How were chores this morning, Ash?" Colton or Pike would ask him over dinner.

And then there was Justice again, waiting like a crouching tiger to pounce when he got home with all sorts of hot and delicious foods.

"I made beef stew *and* chicken stew, Ash," Justice would say. "You can have one or both." Justice was used to cooking for an army of hungry ranchers, but delighted in the challenge of getting to know what the young boy liked and didn't like. And Ash was more than willing to play along.

"I like this lasagna more than that spaghetti, Justice," Ash might say, "but I like this chicken pot pie more than the lasagna."

Justice would take it all in. He liked the boy, and knew he had been sick. The cook made it his goal to cure him with "good eats," and fatten him up.

"Have mercy, Justice," Ash would say, "I can't button my jeans."

At that, Justice would laugh victoriously, and plan the next day's feast.

As for Ash's jeans, Gunnar told him he could walk to the outfitters in town any day after school and buy what he needed. New pants and shirts, boots, a winter coat—and put it all on the West family account.

The first time he did he eyed the door warily, thinking he'd have to make a dash for it if they didn't believe him; if they thought he was stealing. But the woman behind the counter simply smiled and said, "of course, you must be Gunnar's boy."

Gunnar's boy.

"Ash," she continued, "Gunnar said to make sure you don't leave without a warm hat and wool gloves, and long johns too—the first snow is around the corner. And from the looks of it, you need a few more flannel shirts to see you 'til Spring."

WHEN HE FIRST ARRIVED AT THE RANCH, WEAKENED BY THE VIRUS AND heart sick over Granny, Ash stayed in his room a lot. He tried to make himself small and invisible—he'd be no trouble at all, so they'd let him stay. But that plan didn't work.

Justice brought him a few meals in bed, but then urged him to come sit by the fire in the kitchen where he'd be warm. While there, the ranch cook would talk up a storm and bring Ash small plates filled with hot dishes.

Before long the old guy, Ridge West, was sitting across from Ash and pulling up a chess board. After a few tutorials that he never asked for, Ash found himself playing game after game, and actually winning a few. Which made the competitive Ridge want to play even more.

Then there was Colton. At 29, he was the closest to Ash in age. Like a big lumbering puppy, Colton seemed to be waiting his whole life for a younger brother to pal around with. Colton was teaching Ash to drive an old Jeep on the ranch. Gunnar said that after he got his license, he might be able to get to and from school by himself. Though nobody complained about picking Ash up.

Pike was another story. Quiet and more introspective than the other Wests, Pike would often be gone for days at a time, working in the many outer acres of the West land. Ash was beginning to think that Pike didn't care for him at all until one day.

"Ash, quick come here," he heard Pike call him from the great room.

A wave of anxiety hit Ash as he wondered what he'd done to offend the family. Was something missing, and would he be accused? When he nervously followed Pike's voice to the big window, Pike handed him binoculars and pointed to a spot in the distance.

"See that elk in the clearing—that's a Roosevelt Elk. It's rare to spot one, especially this far east," Pike said. "They're darker than the others with massive racks of antlers."

Ash did see the elk, and it was amazing and majestic in its graceful movements.

"Whoa," was all Ash could say.

"*Whoa* is right little buddy," Pike said, and then clapped Ash on the back as he turned to leave the lodge.

That was just Pike's way, Ash figured, and that was okay. He'd gladly be Pike's little buddy, Gunnar's boy, and Colton's kid brother—

all day long. He'd be Ridge's chess opponent, and Justice's guinea pig when it came to sampling his good cooking.

He'd be Kat's sounding board as they took the long drive to and from town, while Kat told him about whatever virus she'd been reading about.

The Wests were kind and generous, hard-working people. And Ash couldn't believe his dumb luck to be living under their roof. If his thieving days weren't behind him, he would have a field day stealing and pawning the valuables that just sat around the ranch—expensive artwork and bronzes, and oil paintings, often stuck in little-used rooms.

He spotted pricey binoculars, antique wrist watches, and leather-bound first edition books. There was a drawer in the kitchen filled with petty cash; hundreds of dollars for unexpected items Justice might need, or to tip a courier at the door.

Ash wasn't even tempted. He had only taken to stealing so he could buy food for his granny. Here, the family saw to his every need. He confessed his trespasses to Gunnar one day, knowing there was a chance the Wests might throw him out. But he couldn't keep it in any longer.

"I want to make it right, but don't know where to begin," Ash said, handing Gunnar the tin box filled with cash that he'd retrieved from Granny's shed.

Gunnar silently took the box and gave him a sad smile. Then he told him that once, long ago, he'd taken his daddy's favorite silver razor to teach himself how to shave. He'd paid dearly for it with all the nicks and cuts in his adolescent face, and could therefore hardly hide his sins from Ridge.

"I ought to tan your hide, Gunnar," Ridge said when he found out, "but I think you've punished yourself quite enough." Ash laughed with Gunnar at the story. He thought it was Gunnar's way of saying that Ash had suffered enough, and it was time to move on.

After school the next day, Gunnar picked the boy up and drove him to the West Gorge Bank where they opened an account in Ash's name—funded with $500 from Gunnar. The teller handed Ash a bank card that he could use to withdraw cash or make purchases.

"I'll add your allowance to the account every month," Gunnar told the speechless boy. "Buy a few things you want—things you can't get at the outfitters. Bring your granny some flowers every now and then. Ladies like that sort of thing."

And then he added, "Ash, we all earn our keep at the ranch, you included; but each of us is there by the grace of God and that's a fact."

Afterwards, Gunnar took Ash up to Cindy's Diner for a burger and a milkshake. And later that night, as Cindy and the waitresses emptied out the shared tip jar as they did every night, they were stunned to find a little tin box, stuffed with hundreds of dollars.

CHAPTER 49

A lot changed for Gunnar in a few months' time, too.

Five a.m. still came just as early, but most mornings were blessedly like this one, where he woke up and heard the shower running in his suite. Inhaling the steam through an open door, it smelled sweet, like honey and apricots.

As the water stopped, Gunnar smiled and stretched out his arms, anticipating the kiss Kat would give him on her way to the dressing room.

He'd cleared half his closet for his bride, and then laughed at how few things she had to hang in it. No matter, it was slowly filling up with new shirts and suede jackets, jeans and boots, and more than one hat for riding the range on horseback.

"Morning, cowboy," Kat said softly as she bent down to kiss Gunnar in the darkened room.

"Morning yourself, sheriff," he said, softly moaning as she kissed him again. He lifted a sleepy hand and caressed her dewy skin, feeling the shiver that shot down her spine.

Kat laughed a little and padded off to the closet with a parting comment. "That sunrise is not going to watch itself, husband," she said.

Moments later, Mrs. Kat West emerged from the dressing room with her hair piled in a curly bun on top of her head. She wore one of Gunnar's shirts with the sleeves rolled up to her elbows. As she walked barefoot towards the kitchen, he took a moment to appreciate his wife's beautiful long legs, then threw the covers back.

His bride was expecting him to join her, and he'd never make her wait.

He had so many favorite parts to his day now, starting with walking into the kitchen and seeing Kat pour two mugs of hot coffee. She was so at home at the ranch, and every morning, as excited as the one before. Together, they'd sit on the big deck with a wool throw and binoculars, watching the gorge and the mountains come into view.

The two of them would sit together long before anyone else was awake and enjoy the sights and sounds of the mountains. Gunnar felt like he was seeing everything for the first time, through her eyes. The hundreds of eagles Gunnar had spotted in his lifetime did not compare to the first one his wife saw from the deck of the ranch.

On cold or rainy mornings, Gunnar would start a fire in the great room, and they would cozy up in one of the oversized leather chairs and gaze out the massive windows, while whispering about their day ahead.

After Kat left for the hospital, Gunnar went about his work with a stupid grin on his face, thinking about how full his heart felt and how sweet his life was. He tried to hide his happiness from the ranch hands and his brothers, but it was hopeless.

Some days, Gunner would come home to find Kat laughing with Ridge about some shaggy dog story his dad loved to tell, or sitting with him in the sunny kitchen and playing a game of chess, while a fire crackled nearby.

Gunnar loved the way his wife and father had become friends. One day, shortly after the wedding, Ridge hinted that maybe he ought to move into one of the guest houses on the property and give the newlyweds some space.

"Never, Ridge," she said emphatically, "and I mean that with all my heart. This is a family home, and you've all been so kind to open your hearts to me. I am in your debt!"

It wasn't long after that when the West patriarch gave his new daughter-in-law an immeasurable gift—he invited her to make Randi's beautiful pine desk her own, and move her medical books onto the shelves, right next to the law journals.

"Randi would want you in this room," Ridge said in a grizzled voice, "I feel that in my bones." Kat hugged Ridge, and told him what an honor that would be. "Thank you, Dad," she said. "It's a beautiful wedding gift."

Kat also became a most loved sister to both Pike and Colton.

When the quiet, introspective Pike discovered Kat's new appreciation of Western art, they began pouring over books and paintings together—reading about Frederic Remington, Charles Russell and James Moran. They planned a few outings to local galleries and museums, inviting Gunnar to come along.

"I'm busy that day," Gunnar said.

"You don't even know what day we're going," Kat responded with a laugh.

"Don't matter—I'm busy," her husband said with a smirk.

No doubt about it, the entire household was energized by the addition of Kat and Ash to the West Ranch. As a family, they had been like a toy that had run out of batteries, collecting dust in a dark corner. Now, there was life and noise, and laughter.

Justice was falling over himself, happy to be preparing family meals once again, instead of just sandwiches for lethargic bachelors. He had Ash in his sights every day and knocked himself out cooking for the boy.

He even enjoyed sharing the kitchen with Kat when she had time —she taught him how to make her favorite leek and swiss cheese quiche, and corn chowder.

"The missus would have loved your cooking," Justice told her, and

Kat thanked him for the compliment. "I will hold that dear to my heart, Justice."

Ridge was smiling again. His sons thought he'd forgotten how. He was smitten with the beautiful doctor who was now his daughter, and the love was reciprocated. Kat was fussing over Ridge, tracking his blood pressure and salt intake. He pretended to be bothered, but Gunnar could tell he felt cared for.

The Wests were coming to life and they had Kat to thank. Because of her, doors that had been closed were opened again. Lamps were turned on. Candles flickered and fires roared. Dinners were served once again on the family ironstone dishes—not just eaten out of a pan.

When November came around, there was general excitement about Thanksgiving. Kat's mother, Trudy, would be flying in to spend the holidays at the ranch. Pike and Colton invited Ash to come with them into the forest to help cut down a tall pine to put in the great room for Christmas. They hadn't put up a tree in years—not since Randi got sick.

As for Kat, she suddenly had so many men in her life that she could count on, each one more dependable than the next, helping her forget how much pain her own father had caused.

There was Ridge, who welcomed her to the ranch with grace and love. Pike and Colton did too—they became the brothers she never knew she needed, but could not imagine living without. Even Justice and Ash could be called true men of honor.

And there was Gunnar. She eagerly slipped into his arms every night, unable to comprehend her good fortune at being loved by this man. And every night he said the same thing as he kissed her tenderly, and whispered into her silky curls.

"I will never leave you nor forsake you."

CHAPTER 50

"*J*will never leave you nor forsake you," Gunnar promised on the day he proposed. Kat thought of that September day often.

She and Gunnar had been inseparable since the day he showed up at her apartment. On this day, he wanted to take her on horseback through some of the more remote West property, before the weather changed to a short fall and early winter.

The day was sunny and beautiful. The aspen leaves shone bright yellow, like gold coins flickering in the breeze. Kat gasped at their loveliness. In the meadow, the Indian Paintbrush flowers had bloomed and gone away, leaving just a ghost of their bright red leaves behind.

Gunnar was unusually quiet, but reached out many times to touch her arm or her hand, or gently rub her leg. He was so dear to her, and she fell more in love with him each day.

As they neared the river, Gunnar got in front of her horse and took the reins, guiding him around a grove of trees. There in a clearing, Kat could see a beautiful table set with white linens, speckled tin plates and champagne flutes.

"What...?" Kat had no words for the vision she was seeing. She was amazed at the mountain picnic Gunnar had planned, and could not imagine all that had gone into his efforts.

"Let's give the horses a rest, shall we?" He helped her down from her horse.

As Gunnar tied the horses to a tree by the river where they could drink the cool water, Kat took a minute to look around her as she stretched her arms and legs, and freed her hair from the hat she had been wearing.

"Kat?" Gunnar was behind her, softly calling her name.

When she turned back, he was bent down on one knee waiting for her.

"Sweet Kat," he said, taking her hand in his.

Tears threatened to spill from Kat's eyes as she took in the sight of her beloved man.

"Will you marry me, Kat?" Gunnar asked in a whisper. He cleared his throat and continued. "Will you be my wife for all of our days? In good and bad, in sickness… and health?"

Kat could not speak. He had taken her breath away.

"I do not know what the future holds, dear girl," Gunnar said, "but I promise, I vow, that I will never leave you nor forsake you. And I'll renew this promise every day."

"Yes, Gunnar," she found herself saying as she fell to her knees and into his arms, "I will be your wife for all of our days."

And in spite of her resolve to not ever again shed a tear over the likes of Gunnar West, tears streamed down Kat's face at the over-whelming devotion she felt for her cowboy.

Still holding her hand, Gunner slid a beautiful gold ring on her finger, set with diamonds and a large opal that caught the sun and refracted light and colors—it was unlike anything she'd ever seen.

Over their lunch at the table by the mountains, they determined that Kat didn't want a big wedding, and Gunnar didn't want a long engagement—so they set a date just weeks away. The ceremony and following luncheon would be held on the grounds of the ranch.

The guest list was small and included Kat's mother, plus Gunnar's father and brothers. Marta and June were there with their husbands, and Jackie and Red seemed happy to be guests, and not the cooks. Justice had that honor to himself, upon his insistence.

Josh Quell came with a pretty young animal doctor from town. And Shep and Arlene glowed with happiness for Kat and Gunnar. As did JaneAnn.

Kat didn't invite any of her old friends from Chicago. "I'll send them a Christmas card," she said with a smile, "from Gunnar and Kat West."

It was time to start a new chapter in her life.

On their wedding day, the early Autumn sun shone brightly. Kat walked down the grassy meadow aisle wearing white lace and carrying a romantic bouquet made from purple Russian sage and eucalyptus, as well as Queen Anne's lace. Her cowboy looked tall and striking in a tailored suit and his best hat.

The walk seemed to take forever but when she reached Gunnar, he took her hand and she took his name. For better or for worse.

When the preacher announced them husband and wife, Gunnar slowly put his hands on her waist, and then wrapped his arms around her, pulling her into him the way she'd become accustomed—making her feel as though he'd never let her go. And when they kissed, they were the only two people in existence.

The kiss went on so long that their guests and the preacher got antsy, and started walking through the meadow towards the food and drink.

Mr. and Mrs. West did not care in the least.

Later, as the guests enjoyed their cake and coffee, Ridge West stood up and clinked his water glass with the tines of his fork. "Everyone," Ridge said to the group, "if I could have just a moment."

When they had quieted down, Ridge went on to welcome Kat and her mother, and Ash, into the West clan. He said that none of their lives, happily, would ever be the same. And then to smiles and tears, Ridge began to tell a story.

"Life is full of surprising and delightful stories," he said, thinking about his own life's story, and how surprised he had been when the beautiful Randi Petersen walked into his life so many years before.

How proud she would be of this day, he knew.

"But few stories are as surprising or as delightful as the time my oldest son, Gunnar, went to the hospital to return a phone, and came home with his family."

LATER THAT DAY, AS THE SUN SET AND GUESTS SAID THEIR FAREWELLS, Gunnar pulled Kat aside and handed her a small velvet box. Inside was a wedding gift, he said, and Kat assumed it was another piece of beautiful jewelry. Gunnar couldn't seem to stop showering her with shiny gifts and she was always delighted.

Instead, it was a shiny key to #22.

He had purchased the condo that she had grown to love. "It's yours alone, Kat West," he said with a smile. "You might want time away from the ranch every now and then; a break from all the men."

"Maybe not *all* the men," Kat said with a smile as she dangled the key. She was thinking how it might be nice to cook dinner for just her husband occasionally, and enjoy time alone with Gunnar—as much as she loved life at the big family home.

"Maybe I can come visit you," Gunnar said playfully.

"Maybe," Kat said, "but be careful. I just might quarantine you, cowboy."

"You do that, sheriff," Gunnar said. Then he kissed his wife.

END

* * *

MORE WEST BROTHERS ROMANCES

Ready for more sweet romance with the West brothers?

Catch up with the rest of the family in the West Brothers Romances 2 - 6!

DRAWING HER COWBOY
A West Brothers Romance #2

Beautiful and rich, Paislee seems to have a perfect life – but she feels like she's losing herself in the smothering grip of her controlling fiancée. So when her grandmother suggests a road trip to unravel a family mystery, she jumps at the chance. She is determined to find answers, and finds more than she bargained for when she follows Pike West to the old settler's barn. Trapped by a blizzard, Paislee is soon wearing a prairie dress and dining by candlelight with the cowboy who caught her imagination. Will he catch her heart, too?

STIRRING HER COWBOY
A West Brothers Romance #3

Life is fun and games for Colton West, until his steamy introduction to ranch's beautiful new cook. But she's a trained chef, not some chuckwagon bean-slinger, and wants Colton to simmer down. When their grizzled old camp cook retires, the last thing Colton expects is to fall in love with his replacement. But when Chef Liu Chen feeds his body and soul, his heart isn't far behind.

Liu is an accomplished and confident fourth-generation Chinese-American. Her parents and grandparents discourage her from falling in love with a cowboy. But Colton is not going down without a fight. And Liu's heart begins to soften toward this man working so hard to earn her love.

HER SUNSET COWBOY
A West Brothers Romance #4

After her lowlife ex took off with all her savings, Casey Parks has to pick herself up and rebuild—and she does so with a vengeance. Her take-no-prisoners attitude is all the fuel she needs to rebuild her Wyoming real estate empire. Until her ambition puts her in a head-on collision with Ridge West - town legend, billionaire benefactor, and major thorn in her side. As the handsome widower sets his sights on her territory, Casey pulls out all her tricks to slow him down—but for how long?

Ridge West is too far down the road for love. At least, that's what he keeps telling himself. But his heart is telling him a different story. Especially when he's anywhere near Casey Parks. She wakes up parts of him that have been asleep for a long time. Even when she's out-bidding, out-maneuvering and undermining his every move. He doesn't even like Casey—he couldn't possibly be falling in love with her...could he?

SASSY COWGIRL KISSES
A West Brothers Romance #5

Sassy worked hard to get her summer internship at West Ranch. She had to – she made a promise and she aims to keep it, even if it drops like a bomb on the ranch hands she cares for. But every time she turns around, a certain cowboy seems to be rescuing her from scrapes and distracting her from her mission. Even his awkward attempts at flirting are cute and disarming.

Finally through with college, Ash West is ready to help run the ranch, but instead he keeps running into their new intern, Sassy. Ash knows that nothing but trouble lies behind Sassy's curves and sparkling smiles, but can't stop dreaming about stealing a kiss from the cowgirl.

First love burns hot for Ash and Sassy and their passion takes them by surprise. But Sassy's secret burns hotter. Can she really rock the West family's world and go home like she planned? Or can she and Ash find happiness after he discovers who she really is?

A WEST RANCH CHRISTMAS
  A West Brothers Romance #6

When Sassy came back to Wyoming and Ash, she promised to stay until Christmas. Ash is giving her space to decide if there's a cowboy in her future, but the twinkling lights and falling snow remind him of the looming deadline. How can he be patient and let their love story unfold, when every instinct tells him to grab Sassy and never let her go?

There's a flurry of activity at West Ranch as the family gets ready for a holiday wedding, complete with a nervous groom, an anxious bride, and the ghosts of girlfriends past. One of the West brothers is expecting a special bundle of Christmas joy, another is hiding a secret that will upend their lives.

Will the Christmas Eve wedding come off without a hitch? Will Ash and Sassy's love story get wrapped up in a beautiful bow? Catch up with the entire West family as they celebrate the Christmas season together. There will be sleigh rides, more than one surprise, and of course snow!

HER UNEXPECTED COWBOY
A free story in the West Brothers Romances

She was looking for a cowboy, not a nerd. Then a dangerous bull moose reveals a cowboy heart beating in the chest of this city slicker.

Click here to download Her Unexpected Cowboy for free. Or go to KathyFawcett.com

OTHER BOOKS BY KATHY FAWCETT

Shoulder Season, Lake Michigan Lodge #1

Kay is finally renovating her life. Now who will she share it with? In this funny uplifting tale of renovation, redemption and romance, a rustic old lodge on Lake Michigan isn't the only thing that gets a second chance.

Water Dance, Lake Michigan Lodge #2

In the second book of the Lake Michigan Lodge Series, can Kay's happy-ever-after survive an invasion of teenage girls?

ABOUT KATHY FAWCETT

Kathy Fawcett is an award-winning advertising writer who has lived most of her life in the state of Michigan. She met her own Wyoming cowboy in college, when they both attended Northern Michigan University. Steve Fawcett introduced the author to his home and family in Wilson, Wyoming, outside of Jackson Hole—and decades later, the two travel there whenever possible. For several years, Kathy lived in suburban Detroit where she raised their three children and enjoyed a busy freelance writing career. Kathy now resides near Lake Michigan. She enjoys camping, kayaking and biking with her husband. Follow the author on Instagram and Facebook, and write Kathy an email at Kathy@kathyfawcett.com – she loves to write back.